## *"How come you're still single?"*
## *Ross asked.*

"Because none of the men I dated met my requirements," Glory said softly. *None of them could compare to you.* She eased closer to him on the prickly hay.

"I take it you've set certain standards for your future husband?" Ross asked, inching away.

"Oh, definitely." Glory smiled in the semidarkness. If he scooted any farther away, he'd be out of the barn! "Any man I married would have to love horses," she said.

"Stands to reason."

"And children," she put in.

Yeah, Ross could see it now. Her parents beaming over the grandkids. But what he couldn't see was some stranger in the family portrait. "What else would you want from this lover of horses and children?"

"He would have to be dependable, loyal and honorable," she answered, smiling.

Loyal and dependable Ross could handle. But what was honorable about the secrets he'd kept from Glory all these years?

Dear Reader:

All of us here at Silhouette Books hope that you are having a wonderful summer, and enjoying all that the season has to offer. Whether you are vacationing, or spending the long, warm summer evenings at home, we wish you the best—and hope to bring you many happy hours of romance.

August finds our DIAMOND JUBILEE in full swing. This month features *Virgin Territory* by Suzanne Carey, a delightful story about a heroine who laments being what she considers "the last virgin in Chicago." Her handsome hero feels he's a man with a mission—to protect her virtue *and* his beloved bachelorhood at the same time. Then, in September, we have an extraspecial surprise—*two* DIAMOND JUBILEE titles by two of your favorite authors: Annette Broadrick with *Married?!* and Dixie Browning with *The Homing Instinct*.

The DIAMOND JUBILEE—Silhouette Romance's tenth anniversary celebration—is our way of saying thanks to you, our readers. To symbolize the timelessness of love, as well as the modern gift of the tenth anniversary, we're presenting readers with a DIAMOND JUBILEE Silhouette Romance each month, penned by one of your favorite Silhouette Romance authors.

And that's not all! This month don't miss Diana Palmer's fortieth story for Silhouette—*Connal*. He's a LONG, TALL TEXAN out to lasso your heart! In addition, back by popular demand, are Books 4, 5 and 6 of DIANA PALMER DUETS—some of Diana Palmer's earlier published work which has been unavailable for years.

During our tenth anniversary, the spirit of celebration is with us year-round. And that's all due to you, our readers. With the support you've given us, you can look forward to many more years of heartwarming, poignant love stories.

I hope you'll enjoy this book and all of the stories to come. Come home to romance—Silhouette Romance—for always!

Sincerely,

Tara Hughes Gavin
Senior Editor

# PEPPER ADAMS

# Cimarron
# Glory

CIMARRON
STORIES

Silhouette Romance

Published by Silhouette Books New York

America's Publisher of Contemporary Romance

SILHOUETTE BOOKS
300 E. 42nd St., New York, N.Y. 10017

ISBN: 0-373-08740-3

First Silhouette Books printing August 1990

Printed in the U.S.A.

**Books by Pepper Adams**

Silhouette Romance

*Heavenly Bodies* #486
*In Hot Pursuit* #504
*Taking Savanah* #600
*Cimarron Knight* #724
*Cimarron Glory* #740

*Cimarron Stories

---

## PEPPER ADAMS

lives in Oklahoma with her husband and children. Her interest in romance writing began with obsessive reading and was followed by writing courses, where she learned the craft. She longs for the discipline of the "rigid schedule" all the how-to books exhort writers to maintain, but does not seriously believe she will achieve one in this lifetime. She finds she works best if she remembers to take her writing, and not herself, seriously.

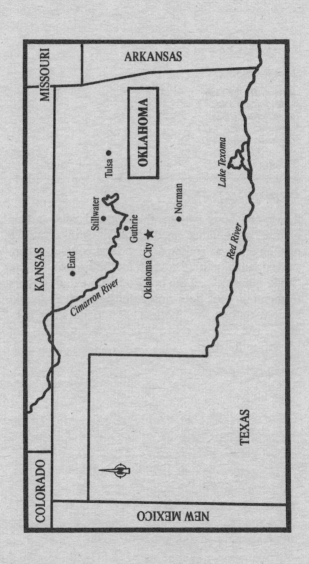

# Prologue

Jeez, it was just a little smooch. Not the crime of the century.'' Glory Roberts was madder than a peeled rattler, and it showed when she slammed the door behind the last of her hastily departing guests. She'd so wanted this party to be special, the perfect showcase for her previously undisplayed seventeen-year-old sophistication.

She had a new short haircut that looked more like New York City than Oklahoma City and a sexy red dress to go with her newly mature outlook on life. She'd been looking forward to tonight for weeks, and now everything was ruined.

Tomorrow she'd be leaving for college—four years of premed and four years of vet school. But she was ready for the challenge. Tonight should have been goodbye, childhood—hello, womanhood. Sacred rites of passage and all that good stuff. Ha!

She turned her brown-eyed fury on the man responsible for turning her big night into the biggest embarrassment of her life. Maybe Ross Forbes was her father's top hand, but he sure as sand fleas wasn't hers. In the four years since he'd turned up at Phoenix Farm, looking for a job, he'd made a careful point of letting her know that he found her about as interesting—and as annoying—as a horsefly.

"Dadgummit, Cocklebur." Glory's favorite name for Ross was not an endearment. "You ruined my party. You had no right butting in and roughing up Larry Dale." She stamped her feet, seriously endangering the three-inch heels on her dyed-to-match pumps.

"Don't cuss, young lady." Ross's quiet order riled her even more.

"I'm an adult now. I can cuss all I want." She cut loose with a few choice expletives she'd heard around the barns, but even those colorful expressions failed to get a reaction out of him. He was just as calm as ever.

She hated calm.

"Is your little temper tantrum over, Brat?" he asked with bored disinterest.

"It's not over until I say it's over, so quit trying to change the subject."

"For your information, I did not *rough up* your precious Larry Dale. I just directed him back into the house where all the fun was. It's his fault if he had his heart set on some private party games in the rose garden."

Glory flushed and her skin tried to compete with her dress in the redness department. "What I do is no business of yours. And even if it was, you didn't have to manhandle him."

"I thought I was plumb gentle. Didn't I pick him up from the ground and dust him off?"

"*After* you manhandled him," she ground out.

"Only his pride was hurt. I can't help it if the boy's as clumsy as a big-footed hound when he's in a hurry."

"He wouldn't have been in a hurry if you hadn't threatened him. Jeez, you're worse than Daddy. At least he trusts me enough to make himself scarce tonight."

Ross nodded. "Yeah. But your daddy has a twisted sense of humor, and he recruited me to chaperon your little tea party."

"Chaperon? Is that what you're supposed to be?" Gone were all thoughts of maturity and sophistication, and Glory yelled at Ross as she had so many times over the years. "So why in blue blazes were you acting like a bouncer?"

"Same difference." He shrugged, and his work-developed muscles strained the fabric of his starchy western shirt.

"I don't need a bodyguard, and I sure don't need a chaperon," she snapped, fists on her hips.

Ross's level gaze held hers. If ever a girl's virtue needed protecting, it was Glory's. In the past six months she'd filled out, ripened with curves and grace. Her sweet-looking, dimpled facade often mislead people into thinking she was as soft as she looked. They were always surprised when they learned her spirit was composed of nine parts steel.

She'd been thirteen the first time he saw her; a ponytailed, blue-jeaned, horse-crazy tomboy who smelled more like her favorite animals than a girl. Her innate skill with horses had earned her the respect of the other ranch hands, but because she was who she was and he was who he was, Ross had tried to stay as far away from her as the lush, well-tended confines of Phoenix Farm allowed.

He'd met with only limited success, because Glory had attached herself to him like the stubborn cocklebur she called him, dogging his trail like a pure nuisance. All they had in common was their love for quarter horses, but still it had taken some serious ignoring to discourage her. He'd been relieved when she'd finally discovered boys her own age.

He saw now that the funny-faced little tomboy was gone forever. In her place was a budding teenage temptress who wasn't even remotely aware of her effect on men. She was the indulged, late-in-life only child of a man wealthy enough to humor her every whim, and she was accustomed to getting her way. But not this time. There wouldn't be any slap and tickle in the garden while he was in charge. Glory wasn't ready for any trips down the primrose path.

Not that she didn't have a healthy appreciation of the biological facts of life. A curious girl didn't grow up on a breeding station without a thorough understanding of both the mating and birth processes. She wasn't ignorant about what went where and why, but emotionally she was a wide-eyed innocent. Ross wasn't about to let some young buck like Larry Dale Toliver hurt her and steal what she was too young to give. Someday she'd meet a man worthy of her.

"Will you please explain why you jumped on poor Larry Dale and scared off all my guests?" Glory demanded.

"Dub told me to look after you and make sure no hanky-panky went on tonight. I take my responsibilities seriously. You should know that."

He was laughing at her and that made her burn brighter. "I am not, nor will I ever be, your responsibility, Ross Forbes. Why can't you get that through your thick head?"

"See, Brat, it's like this," he explained quietly. "When I came here looking for work, your daddy asked me if I was willing to do anything, even the dirtiest job on the place. I was so desperate I said 'sure,' so Dub handed me a shovel. My first job was mucking out the stable."

"So? What's that got to do with anything?"

"When he told me to take care of you tonight, I just gritted my teeth and remembered all the crap I'd already handled on his behalf and here I am."

She smiled in spite of herself and felt her anger easing off. "Daddy's good at manipulating."

"That's not a very nice thing to say."

"Oh, I mean it in a good way. He does it with the horses, too. Remember that mean stallion, Mister Miser? None of you guys could hold him, but all Daddy had to do was walk into the barn and old Miser became a perfect gentleman."

"He's just trustworthy. Animals—and people—sense that."

As maddening as he was, Ross did have his good qualities, Glory admitted. One of those was his relationship with her father. He loved the old horseman as much as she did. "I'm still mad at you. I'll probably never see Larry Dale again after the way you treated him tonight."

"Don't lose any sleep over it," Ross said with a laugh. "There'll be plenty of boys at the university. Fortunately, Larry Dale Toliver, the mental giant, won't be among 'em."

She glared at him and headed for the kitchen with a stack of punch cups. Jeez, it wasn't as if she couldn't take care of herself, she knew how to handle boys. It was just that it gave her a heady sense of power to know that she, Glory Roberts, otherwise known as the Brat with a capital *B*, could tempt a man. Even one as god-awful green as Larry Dale.

She sighed noisily as she stacked the dishes in the sink. "Now I'll never know."

"Know what?" Ross asked suspiciously.

"What it's like to be kissed."

"Is that a fact? What do you call what you were doing behind your mama's rosebushes?"

"Oh, I don't mean kissed." She puckered her lips and smacked the air. "I mean *kissed*." She lowered her voice, hugged herself and moved her mouth like a femme fatale in ecstasy. "Kissed as in till your brains are sucked out."

Ross laughed. "You don't mean kissed, you mean—"

"Never mind what I mean," she said quickly. She wasn't about to talk to him about something as intimate as her desire to become a woman in every sense of the word. In a rush of sentimentality, she said, "I'm sure going to miss this place."

"It won't be the same without you and that's a fact."

"It won't?" she asked hopefully. Even if she was mad at Ross, she couldn't help noticing how sexy he looked.

"No. It'll be peaceful."

For a moment, his eyes challenged hers with the kind of look Glory imagined a man might give a women he found desirable. Before she could figure out what to do about it, he looked away.

Maybe Ross was too blind to see that she wasn't a kid anymore, but *she* didn't have any problems with her sight. Why, she could actually *feel* the virility rolling off him and clogging up the airways. Tonight he was brushed and polished, smelling of some spicy after-shave. His thick brown hair was cut short on the sides, but it was longer in back and almost brushed his collar. His firm jaw was darkened by a perpetual five-o'clock shadow, and he had a little dent on his right cheek that didn't quite qualify as a dimple.

That little dent twitched when he tried to hide his smile as he was doing now. He didn't realize it, but the twitch always gave away the good humor he covered up with macho indifference.

His snug-fitting black jeans had creases so sharp a girl could cut herself on them if she was lucky enough to get that close. The little pearl snaps on his white western shirt would come apart with satisfying ease if someone—some totally out-of-control woman, that is—wanted to rip it off him in a hurry.

He'd rolled up his cuffs, and Glory was fascinated by the golden brown hair on his forearms. She'd seen him working without a shirt and knew those same hairs grew in a thick mat on his chest. His work made him strong, but his strength wasn't all in his muscles. He was smart. Sensitive, too. But old Cocklebur would rather have his eyeballs fried in bear fat than admit that.

All in all, he was a helluva specimen. A girl could do a lot worse than have a man like Ross Forbes teach her about life's little mysteries. "You know what your problem is?"

"Yeah," he muttered. "I'm too refined. I should've kicked Larry Dale's butt."

"Brute. Your problem is you have no romance in your soul."

"It ain't the soul that needs romancin'. A rancher's daughter ought to know that."

"Give me my illusions." With stunning clarity, Glory realized something that she'd known for some time now. She wanted more than illusions from Ross. She wanted reality. And life's little mysteries.

Turning to him, she assumed a provocative tone. "I need to talk to you. It's important."

"With you, it always is. Step into my office." Ross opened the back door that led out onto a big screened-in porch. The sultry night hummed with cicadas, and over at the pond, a couple of dozen bullfrogs were tuning up for a big concert later.

With a plan of seduction only half-formed in her mind, Glory stepped up against Ross, boldly insinuating her body between his and the door. She looked deeply into his eyes and hoped hers conveyed that lambent look so widely favored by centerfold models.

"I'm leaving first thing tomorrow morning," she reminded him.

"I know." Ross tried to ease around her.

"Stillwater's not that far away, but it might as well be on the moon. I'll be too busy studying to come home most weekends. I might not see you again until Thanksgiving."

"That's what I figured."

"I'm going to miss you," she said meaningfully.

"Not for long." Ross backed up a step and encountered the porch swing. "You'll make new friends."

"Not like you. You're special."

"I thought I was an overbearing brute."

Glory ignored that. "*We're* special." She pushed him down onto the swing, and the rusty chains creaked. Taking his hand in hers, she pressed it into the small space between her breasts. "Don't you feel what I feel?"

Ross's heart was thumping worse than a one-legged clogger, and his nerves were shot. Lately he'd been fighting this forbidden attraction. Denying his feelings, disowning his responses until he was nearly unstrung. But fight it he would, because he couldn't afford any more bad choices. The one eight years ago had been a humdinger, and he meant to be living proof that man did indeed learn from his mistakes.

Glory leaned down and braced her hands on top of his thighs. This couldn't be happening to him. He was a twenty-six-year-old man with the experience of one twice his age, and she was a seventeen-year-old girl with the experience of one *half* hers.

Aside from the difference in their ages, there was something else—something dark and immutable—that stood between them like the shadow of a mountain too high to climb. His past. Unforgiving and unrelenting, it was a shameful secret he could never share with anyone as trusting as Glory. Because of what he'd done and what he'd been, he would never be good enough for her.

"Maybe you ate too many hot dogs or something," he suggested as he drew his hand away from her breast and tried to get out of the swing. "Try some antacid."

Before he could escape, Glory threw herself boldly onto his lap, wrapped her arms around his neck in an untutored embrace and pulled his lips down to hers. The kiss was an innocent yet unmistakably passionate challenge. It was impossible to resist, too powerful to deny.

For a crazy suspended-in-time moment Ross forgot about everything but the sweet joy of Glory. He wrapped her in his arms and laid claim to her tender lips. She opened her mouth to him, her tongue timidly parrying with his own. His moist, firm lips moved deliberately over hers, demanding, giving. She moaned and wriggled on his lap and sighed as he learned the taste of her. She might be young and innocent, but her fledgling passions were thoroughly aroused.

Ross's preceptions were single-mindedly focused on the sweet girl in his arms, on the streams of desire that made his whole body tremble. When a sexy little groan escaped her and she squirmed on his lap, he tore his lips away. Burying his face in her neck, he kissed the hollow at the base of her throat. All he could think was that for one so inexperienced, she was a damn quick study.

"I want you, Ross," she whispered. "I want you to love me and teach me how to love you. I want to belong to you."

Ross groaned as though he'd been shot with a .22. A man could only take so much. Impossible reality intruded on the moment, and he hated himself for succumbing to the hunger that had gnawed at him for months. Denying it once more, he pulled away and abruptly set her aside.

He stumbled out of the swing and leaned against the porch railing. Taking a deep breath, he raked a hand through his hair. God, he'd almost lost it! He'd almost broken his promise to her father. He recalled a day, about a year after he'd hired on. He'd approached Dub Roberts about cosigning for a pickup truck he wanted to buy. Normally Ross didn't ask for help, but he'd had no choice. No banks would loan him money on his own word.

Dub had agreed without hesitation. "Hell, kid," he'd said. "I guess I can trust you, you haven't run off with the silver yet. Anything I got is yours."

Glory had ridden by then, a bareback Godiva in cutoff jeans. Her long, tanned legs and budding figure hinted at the butterfly struggling to burst the cocoon of adolescence.

"Anything but my daughter, that is," Dub had amended. "I'll tell you what I tell all the hands. Stay away from my baby." Grateful for the chance Dub had given him, Ross had obeyed that order in thought and deed until tonight.

"Get back over here, Ross Forbes," Glory commanded in a voice much steadier than his had been. "We're not through."

"Oh, yes, we are."

Never having learned the art of deception, self or otherwise, Glory couldn't contain the feelings that filled her to bursting. Ross had noticed her. He'd kissed her like a man kissed a woman. Her happiness squeezed out what control she still possessed.

"Oh, Ross, I love you," she blurted. She jumped up to join him at the railing, and when she tried to put her arms around him again, he sidestepped smartly.

"No, you don't." His voice was tense, gruff. "You're a kid. You don't know what you're saying so don't throw that word around. You love horses and strawberry ice cream and kittens. That's the only kind of love you understand."

Tears welled up in Glory's eyes. "This is different."

"No. You're all caught up in this evening, drunk with the excitement of leaving home. You're still a baby."

"Look at me, Ross." She stood up proudly before him, her firm young breasts heaving inside the low-cut bodice of her too-grown-up dress, her golden skin turned silver in the moonlight. "Do I look like a baby to you?"

"Wearing sexy clothes doesn't make you a woman. Get in the house like a good little girl. In a week or so you'll meet some fresh-faced Aggie and forget all about me."

"You're wrong, Ross. I won't forget." She thought she detected a note of sadness in his voice, and a lone tear spilled down her cheek. "I'll never forget you or this night or our kiss. Ever."

Ross gripped the railing so his hand couldn't reach out to brush the tear away.

"I do love you," she whispered as though afraid the bullfrogs might hear. "It might not mean much to you now, but someday it will. Someday you'll want me, too."

Ross knew he was doing the right thing. Glory would get over her childish crush. "Trust me. By this time next week you'll swear you're in love with someone else and I'll be relegated to the ice-cream and kitten category."

"You kissed me back," she insisted. "You were wanting and needing as much as me. I didn't imagine that."

"Look, Brat, you've been sashaying around here for years trying to get me to notice you. Okay, I noticed. But don't kid yourself into thinking I could ever be interested in a child like you." Finding the words was hard, but making his voice cold and harsh was the toughest thing Ross had ever done. And God knows, he'd done some pretty awful things.

"I'm a man, even if I am just a hired hand. I'm not some peachy-cheeked boy to be satisfied with a slow dance and a few chaste kisses in the garden. If I wanted anything tonight, it was a woman. Not a little girl."

"Don't be angry with me, Ross." Glory felt the emptiness growing like a vacuum inside her. "I love you so much. I've always loved you. Even when I hated you, I loved you."

"Stop making a fool of yourself. If you know what's good for you, you'll get in that house." Ross paused, and when she made no move to obey, he bellowed, "Now."

"But, Ross..."

"You wanna know something else? You look ridiculous. That haircut makes you look like a damn boy!"

Glory finally fled, but not before the tears had flowed and the hurt had burst out of her in great racking sobs. Ross didn't know it yet, but someday they'd finish what she'd started tonight.

In spades.

# Chapter One

Glory Roberts liked surprises as much as the next person, but this one was getting a little out of hand. Wearing a red bandanna blindfold and stumbling around in the dark just wasn't dignified. As a newly licensed D.V.M., with extra research and study behind her, she had a professional image to uphold. How would it look if one of her patients, or rather one of her patients' owners, came in and caught her playing blindman's bluff?

"Lighten up," she reprimanded herself. "Be a good sport and let Mama and Daddy have their fun." She tried to take her own advice, but she was too jumpy to stand still. It seemed as if she'd been waiting for one thing or another all her life.

At age twelve, she'd decided to become a horse doctor, but she'd had to wait years before she was old enough to tackle that dream. She'd plowed through years of study, knowing that when they were over she would return to Phoenix Farm as a resident vet, working alongside her adored and adoring parents.

With characteristic honesty, she admitted that her parents weren't the only reason she'd been eager to come back. She had an ulterior motive—a tall, quiet, hazel-eyed motive.

Ross Forbes. Just thinking about him increased her excitement. Today, with all the sense of accomplishment and homecoming it entailed, had been a long time coming. She didn't want to postpone it a moment longer.

Her parents had picked her up at Will Rogers airport and lavished her with stored-up hugs and kisses. They'd all talked a mile a minute on the way home, and she was barely in the front door before they tied a bandanna around her eyes and whisked her back out into the late winter chill. They'd laughed and giggled like second-graders as they'd led her around, then deposited her here.

But where was here? One of the barns? She sniffed the lightly pine-scented air. No way. She'd spent half her life in horse barns, and she was on intimate terms with that particular odor. It didn't occur to her to sneak a peek at her surroundings since she'd crossed her heart and promised not to. Besides, she had strict orders to stay put. And she always obeyed her daddy.

Sure she did. She reached out, arms groping in front of her, and tested the air on one side and then the other. She thought she heard something, but when she cocked her head and listened, the rustling was gone.

"Okay, who's there?" she called. No one answered.

She kicked off her shoes for balance and hiked up her short tight skirt for mobility. Uncaring that such strenuous movements might reveal more than she wanted to reveal, she stretched her right leg out experimentally. When she encountered no obstacles, she raised it higher and felt around. So far, so good. She took another step. Nothing. *Where was she?*

Glory heard something behind her then and quickly smoothed her black leather skirt down her hips. She didn't have time to worry about the source of the noise, for a door suddenly opened to announce the noisy return of her parents.

"We're back, Gloryhoney." She smiled at the way her mother made one word out of two. "I'm sorry we took so long," Ruby Roberts said breathlessly. "But I forgot something and I want everything to be perfect for you. Now, Dub," she directed her husband, "don't you dare take off that blindfold until I tell you to, hear?"

"I ain't deaf, Mama." Dub hugged Glory and whispered, "That old woman's been ordering me around like a damn drill sergeant for forty years. I guess that's what I get for marryin' an army brat."

"Dubhoney, you wouldn't have it any other way and you know it." She bustled around for a moment. "Okay, you can take off the blindfold now."

Dub removed the bandanna with an excited flourish, and he and Ruby trilled in unison, "Ta-a-a Da-a-a."

It took a moment for Glory's eyes to adjust to the bright interior light. Once they did, she still couldn't believe what she saw. Her parents had updated and remodeled the breeding rooms, enlarged the clinic. The white walls were freshly painted, the slate-gray tile floor highly polished. Recessed lighting played brightly over gleaming countertops and shone on cabinets full of medical supplies.

Everything was brand spanking new, right down to state-of-the-art ultrasound equipment. Dub led her proudly to a tastefully decorated office with her name painted in bold black letters on the door. GLORY ROBERTS—DOCTOR OF VETERINARY MEDICINE. Framed photos of Glory with famous horses born and bred at Phoenix Farms lined the walls with a space reserved for her diplomas and license.

Walnut bookcases held her medical texts as well as her worn copies of *Black Beauty*, *National Velvet* and *A Girl's Anthology of Favorite Horse Stories*. There was a special shelf to display the countless show ribbons and riding trophies she'd won throughout her long love affair with horses. On the wide walnut desk sat a basket of hothouse azaleas in the deep pink color she favored.

"That's what I forgot," Ruby explained. "Read the card."

Glory's hand trembled as she removed the card from the tiny envelope. "You've done us proud" was scrawled in her father's familiar hen scratch. She looked up, her eyes misted with tears of happiness.

"Are you surprised, Gloryhoney?" her mother asked.

"That's putting it mildly. When you two stage a surprise, you really pull out the stops, don't you?"

"Hey, nothin' is too good for the place where my daughter the doctor hangs out her first shingle." Dub clutched her in a bear hug. At five foot eight, she was an inch taller than he was.

"But the expense. All this stuff must have cost a fortune."

"Don't worry about that," her father dismissed. "You'll earn it. Thanks to good management, Phoenix Farm has expanded so much we need a resident vet. Having one on call just doesn't cut it now."

Glory was exclaiming over the shining new fixtures when she saw him. Ross. The prime player in her childhood dreams and her grown-up fantasies. He was her father's ranch manager now and largely responsible for Phoenix's success. His broad shoulders were braced nonchalantly against the wall as if he had nothing better to do. If the truth was known, he'd probably rather be anywhere than here at this moment. He'd made it his job to avoid her for years.

Glory couldn't stop looking at him. Ross was even more tempting than she remembered, but he'd changed. For one thing, he'd grown a mustache. The long silky sweep of it was an appealing addition to his deeply tanned face, as were the fine character lines of rugged maturity. He still had the look of the outdoors about him, still had the light of far horizons in his intense hazel eyes.

She hadn't seen much of him while she was away at school. She'd been too absorbed in her studies to make many trips home, and it had been easier for Dub and Ruby to visit her. She'd spent the last semester working on a research grant at the University of California at Davis. She hadn't seen her family at all during that time, but they'd strengthened their close ties with weekly letters and long chatty phone calls.

Ross had been busy, too. Over the years he'd moved up from stable mucker second-class to the highest position on the farm. She knew all about his success. Dub and Ruby had filled her in about his progress, just as she knew they must have bored him to death with hers. Through them she learned of his innovative ideas to expand the operation with well-planned additions. She knew secondhand of the savvy way he dealt with clients and that his unrelenting honesty had earned him a fine reputation in the business.

Dub and Ruby were as proud of Ross as they were of their foster sons, Brody and Riley Sawyer, and they never tired of talking about him. Glory had always listened with interest to their home-front reports, but her biggest fear had been that one day they'd tell her Ross was getting married.

Something must be wrong with the women in Oklahoma, because he should have been snatched up years ago. It was the natural progression of things. Brody married last fall, and Noelle was just what her tough old brother had needed to soften him up. Riley had married young, but that hadn't worked out, and Glory hoped that he would meet someone, too. He deserved a second chance with a special woman who really cared about him.

For nearly nine years she'd braced herself for the dreaded news that Ross had taken a wife. But by some miracle it hadn't come. If there were women in his life, and there surely were, because a man didn't look like Ross Forbes and not attract women, he kept his personal affairs private. According to Ruby's latest report, he did not have a significant other.

Yet.

He'd always been good-looking, but now that the years had settled on him like a soft-worn denim shirt, he was downright compelling. The deceptive laziness of his slouching stance hid a latent aggressiveness that was intensely sensual. His worn jeans fit him in a blatant declaration of his sex and molded to his muscular thighs and slim hips. The lean hardness of his body did not come from working out. It came from working.

He was the same, only more so. Maybe he hadn't really changed at all. Maybe she was the one who was different. For the first time since he'd drifted onto the place that hot August day, she was viewing him through a woman's eyes. She liked what she saw.

In mere seconds, almost nine years of maturity and experience fell away and Glory was a giddy, hopeless teenager again. With no more control than that of a sparrow caught in a twister, she was drawn by the same macho magnetism that attracted others to him.

Men trusted him because he was one of the guys. Tough and dependable, Ross was the kind of man they wanted on their side when trouble came. Women sensed his hidden pain and longed to comfort him, to try to take the deep-down sadness out of his eyes.

"Welcome home, Brat," Ross said finally. The tightness that had clamped around his throat the moment he'd walked in and caught Glory unaware made talking difficult. He'd meant to announce his presence right off, but when she hiked up her skirt and exposed those long gorgeous legs, he'd lost the power to communicate. What really did him in was the glimpse he'd had of silk rose-pink panties. One look at those and he was a goner.

"It's good to be back."

"You've grown up," he said, stating the obvious.

"Nice of you to notice."

"I noticed a lot of things." Like the way the light teased highlights out of the long brown hair tumbling to her shoulders. The way her black leather suit showed off her lithe figure. The way her angel's face and just-right curves added up to feminine perfection. Hell, yes, he'd noticed. Glancing at her bare feet, he said, "I see it's true what they say about taking the girl out of the country."

In her pleasure at seeing Ross again, Glory had forgotten about her discarded shoes. "Can't take the country out of the girl," she agreed with a mischievous grin as she slipped on her pumps.

Ross had tried to bow out of this homecoming celebration the same way he'd avoided all but the most superficial contact with Glory in the past. But Dub and Ruby had been disappointed. Since he couldn't refuse them anything they asked, he'd finally agreed, figuring that after so many years things had probably changed.

Glory wasn't the same girl who'd spent her youth trying to attract his attention. The four years between his arrival at Phoenix Farm and her departure from it had been filled with verbal jousts and keen competition. Her volatile personality had always had the same effect on his serious one as a flint had on steel, sparking constant tension and conflict. Aware that his nerves were drawn tighter than a bowstring, he decided that maybe things hadn't changed so much after all.

When Glory looked into Ross's smiling eyes, she knew he'd been in the room when she'd thought herself alone and had seen her blind tightrope walk across the clinic floor. He'd probably seen her underwear. She'd looked forward to this meeting for a long time and planned to impress him with her style, dazzle him with her wit. Showing him her drawers, at least at this early stage of the game, was not part of the plan.

"I bet you did notice a lot of things," she said with a wry smile that told him what she thought of Peeping Toms. She meant to tease him, but something in the hungry way he watched her quickened her pulse and made it impossible to follow through with the gibe. His steady gaze bore into hers, and his mouth quirked in the way she remembered, one corner disappearing into his mustache. The grin had always made her think he knew something she didn't.

Yep, he'd definitely seen her underwear.

"What's this?" he teased. "Glory Jo Roberts at a loss for words?"

"We better call Dan Rather," Dub put in.

Glory just smiled. It felt good to slip into the old banter, to pick up where she'd dropped off. It made it easier to hide the fact that a very heavy-duty something had charged up the air between her and Ross. Maybe she was the only one who felt it, and until she figured out what she was going to do about it, she preferred to keep it to herself. It had taken a long time to get over the hateful things he'd said the night before she'd gone away. Feeling her body's reaction to him now, she wondered if she was over them yet.

Glory squared her shoulders, determined to behave in an adult manner. She'd show Ross how sophisticated she'd become. How impervious she was to his sexy country charm. Hoping no one noticed the sham, she laughed lightly and crossed the room to greet him properly.

"That's no way to welcome a lady home, Ross." Her arms curved naturally around his neck, and she rose on tiptoe for a homecoming kiss. She heard the sharp intake of his breath, felt the tremor that passed through him like an electric shock when she touched him.

The soft brush of his mustache on her lips and the brief taste of his warm mouth was a heady sensation. She was shocked by her ready response. It was as if her sleeping senses had suddenly awakened with an intense need to experience all they'd missed in his absence.

Drawn into the unexpected embrace, Ross clamped his hands reflexively around her waist to maintain a decent, and necessary, distance. Torn between the desire to gather her close and the fear of doing so, he closed his eyes and willed away the urge to kiss his way down her neck, her shoulders, her— Regaining some composure, he pretended he didn't want her at all. Which wasn't too difficult, considering he'd had years of practice doing just that.

Before Glory could do little more than brush her lips across his, Ross set her away from him like a hot poker that he'd picked up by mistake. Outwardly he seemed unaffected, but she sensed that even the brief caress had played havoc with his libido.

"I hope you don't plan to greet all the hands like that," he said with a false indifference. "If you do, I won't get any work out of them the rest of the day."

Despite his attempts to hide his feelings, Glory's smile told him she knew exactly what she'd done to him. The glint of triumph in her eyes said she reveled in the knowledge. She hadn't changed as much as he'd thought. She was still the same old Glory, bold and full of fire. As impulsive as she was curious, she'd always been eager to explore new territory. Forbidding her anything only made her want it more.

He recognized a challenge when he saw one. The only difference was, she wasn't a kid anymore, and it wouldn't be easy to ignore. She was an unlikely combination of femininity and toughness, an intriguing woman who knew what she wanted and had the courage to go after it. Making a place for herself in a traditionally male-dominated profession like equine medicine proved that.

The attraction was still there, and the battle to fight it would be more difficult now. But fight it, he must. Touching her even briefly had brought back haunting memories of another time, another kiss. Even then she'd had a power over him. A power that would have been dangerous in her inexperienced hands if he hadn't put an end to it that night on the porch.

He hadn't been right for her then and he wasn't right for her now. All the time in the world wouldn't change that. Maybe the years didn't make that much difference, but the mileage sure did.

Ross knew it was a mistake to place too much importance on a damn kiss. Past or present. More than likely, he'd mistaken the spark of humor in her eyes for something else. That little peck had meant nothing to her, but if he allowed it to, it might mean far too much to him.

"Ross?" Ruby touched his arm.

"Sorry, Ruby." He was embarrassed that he'd been so caught up in his own reverie that he'd almost forgotten there were other people present. "I was just thinking I need to get back to work. Wade Prescott from Tulsa will be here soon with his stallion. High Flyer will be standing at stud for the rest of the season," he explained to Glory. "I'd better check and make sure Harvey has everything ready."

"You've had to double-check Harvey a lot lately," Dub observed.

"Yeah," Ross agreed. "It's getting to be a nuisance. I've given him fair warning. If he doesn't shape up, he's out of here." He didn't like to fire men, but he liked loafers and shirkers even less.

"Oh, I plumb forgot," Ruby exclaimed. "Prescott called and postponed until tomorrow. I guess with the excitement of Glory coming home today and all, it just slipped my mind."

"No problem. Tomorrow's fine." Ross turned to Glory. "Is there anything else you need for the clinic?"

She glanced around at the facility that any vet, first year or twentieth, would be proud of. She still couldn't believe it was hers. "Nope. You all thought of everything." She squeezed her mom and dad. "I have the sweetest, most generous parents in the whole wide world."

"Isn't she quick?" Ross drawled. "It only took her eight years of college to figure that out."

"Now you behave, Ross Forbes," Ruby scolded gently. "Don't you go teasing Glory on her first day home. She's been away a long time, so let her get used to you again, gradual like."

"I'll behave, but only because you asked me to." Ross put his arm around the older woman's shoulders and kissed the top of her head. "She's right, you know. She does have the most generous parents in the world. And the sexiest mother."

Ruby blushed to the roots of her gray hair, and her sun-toughened face dissolved in wrinkles of merriment. She wiggled out of Ross's embrace and punched him on the arm. "Hey, handsome, I thought I told you not to kiss me in front of my husband. It might give him ideas." She glanced at Dub, then winked and turned her wrinkled lips up to Ross's impudently. "On second thought, do that again."

Everyone laughed as Ross obliged. "Dub, will you get this dirty old woman off me? I've got a lot of work to do."

Watching the friendly interplay between her parents and Ross, Glory couldn't help feeling a bit left out. The three of them had shared more of one another's time than she had, but she planned to make up for that now that she was home for good.

"You'll be at the house later for dinner, won't you?" she asked Ross hopefully. Her mother was planning a special meal for the family to celebrate her homecoming.

"I'll be there. Ruby feeds me regularly. She's afraid I'll kill myself if left to my own devices. Have her tell you about the time I blew up a plastic bowl full of chili in the microwave." He mussed Glory's hair playfully as he passed, because he couldn't bear not to touch her in some way.

"About my teasing," he said softly, "no hard feelings." None that he could talk about, he thought with a slow smile.

Glory watched him stride away, his hips swinging in the loose manner of horsemen, and sighed in exasperation. Dang Ross Forbes anyhow! She never had been able to read his poker-faced expressions, and today had been no exception. She'd made a fool of herself once by throwing herself at him, and it looked as though she'd almost repeated the mistake. What was the man made of—stone?

She'd always imagined that he cared for her, that somewhere inside his tough-guy exterior he had a heart and that she might even occupy a small place in it. Evidently that was the only place her feelings were reciprocated—in her imagination. Had the loneliness of the long years of separation led her to create a bond that simply wasn't there? What had their relationship been?

Not friends. The gap in their ages was too great for that. Ross hadn't let her get close enough for true friendship to develop, had never shared the details of his life before Phoenix Farm. Neither had he adopted a big-brother attitude like Brody and Riley had. Besides, what she felt for Ross could in no way be termed sisterly.

All through her teen years she had idolized him, but the night she'd offered him her love, he'd pushed her away and called her a little fool. Had he meant what he said that night, or was his rejection based on some misguided sense of chivalry? In many ways, Ross was terribly old-fashioned, which made her attraction to him even crazier. He was too opinionated, too stubborn and far too bossy for a modern career-minded woman like herself.

Later, when she was alone unpacking in her old room, she attempted to examine her feelings in a realistic manner. She decided her female pride had been injured when Ross had rebuffed her yet again. Jeez, after all these years, she should be used to it.

She'd been turning down come-ons for nine years, so maybe this was fate's perverse way of showing her what it was like to be on the other side of the rejection. While earning her degrees, she hadn't felt she could afford the distractions of college romances and all the time-consuming game playing they entailed. She'd pulled a 4.0 average through most of premed school by defining her priorities early and by making sure her social life stayed at the bottom of the list.

When she got to vet school, she had even less time to devote to extracurricular activities. There were only twenty-seven such schools in the nation, and they accepted only one out of every six-to-ten qualified applicants. Competition for the limited spaces was too fierce for any but the most serious students.

She'd had her share of dates, but they'd left her feeling empty and dissatisfied. Making love and *being* in love went hand in hand as far as she was concerned, and she'd just never been able to work up the enthusiasm she thought a girl in love should feel. That's why she was probably the world's oldest virgin. Seeing Ross again had made her proud of the title.

And kissing him had allayed her fears that the seed of her sensuality—which had budded prematurely that night on the porch and then withered under the frost of Ross's rejection—had completely died from lack of nurturing. It was there, all right. Waiting.

At the expense of her personal life, she'd focused all her energy on her professional goals. So far, she'd achieved them. She'd graduated with honors. She had a clinic of her own. Now she could ease up and think about the future. She could try to make her long-neglected personal life as satisfying as her professional one.

She was confident of her ability to juggle work and family commitments and knew no reason why she couldn't have the kind of loving, teamworking union her parents had. Her father had jokingly pointed out on the drive home from the airport that it was high time she found a man she could love, honor and manage.

She didn't know about the manage part, but Ross fit the other two categories nicely. The trouble was, he was too hardheaded to recognize a good thing when he saw it. She'd learned a long time ago that he couldn't be pushed or prodded, but surely even old Cocklebur himself was vulnerable to subtle seduction. Or was he?

She dressed for supper in a glittery sweater and black slacks, eye-catching but understated. She took extra pains with her makeup and fluffed her hair to disheveled perfection. She'd worn it long ever since Ross had remarked about the androgynous effect short hair had on her. While practicing sultry looks in the mirror, she decided to breeze into that dining room and flat pull the rug out from under Ross Forbes's ostrich-hide boots.

He'd never know what hit him.

She was halfway down the stairs when she realized she'd left her confidence back in her room. She'd never flirted or practiced calculated temptation before, so why did she think she could start at this late date? And in front of an audience yet. Her hand gripped the banister and she stood there, trying to muster up some of the reckless bravado she'd felt earlier.

Even the heavenly smells of her mother's standing rib roast couldn't coax her stomach out of the knots it was tied in. She had to get it together, tonight meant a lot to her parents. Besides, Riley was coming, as well as Brody and Noelle and the kids. She'd missed her family and was eager to spend some time with them.

"Gloryhoney." Her mother's voice drifted in from the kitchen. "Aren't you ready yet?"

"Coming," she answered. What was the matter with her? She was a grown woman, reasonably practical and marginally intelligent. Finding a way to romance the unromanceable Ross Forbes wouldn't be the biggest problem she'd ever tackled.

Not the biggest maybe, she admitted with a secret laugh. But it just might prove to be the most enjoyable.

## Chapter Two

What was meant to be a simple supper turned out to be more like a feast honoring a returning hero, with Glory thrust reluctantly into the title role. She basked in the warm affection and hearty praises of her family and got reacquainted with her brothers and Noelle between the roast beef, au gratin potatoes and the half-dozen salads and vegetables that accompanied all serious country meals.

She smiled at Brody. She'd never seen him so happy. He couldn't take his eyes off his beautiful wife. They'd been married several months and still acted like honeymooners, sharing secret smiles and warm glances when they thought no one was looking. The darkly handsome man and petite blonde made a striking couple, and Glory could only hope to some-day know the kind of fulfillment they had found.

The way they competed for Brody's attention, it was obvious that Noelle's five-year-old twins, Dusty and

Danny, worshiped their stepfather. Brody was enthusiastic about his new role, reacting with patience and affection to their boisterous little-boy ways. Glory wasn't surprised that her oldest brother was a good father, his warmth and humor and unstinting affection had gotten her through plenty of then-serious adolescent crises.

Riley was more outrageous than Brody, but just as endearing in his own way. He'd always looked up to his older brother, his champion and protector. First, after the boys' mother died and then later when their father's abandonment had placed them in a series of foster homes. By the time the Sawyer boys found a permanent home with the Robertses, Riley had adjusted to following his brother's lead.

Riley had had a rough time after his divorce and the subsequent loss of contact with his ex-wife's children from her previous marriage. His quiet depression had worried the whole family. In his despair, he'd withdrawn from the people who loved him and had eventually turned to the numbing effects of alcohol to cope with his pain. He'd sunk so gradually into a private hell that few outside the family had noticed the change in him. Finally, with Brody's support and his own strong will, Riley acknowledged his problem and sought professional help.

No one spoke of those dark days when he had teetered on the brink of self-destruction, because they shared Dub's optimistic belief that the past was over and done with. It was the here and now that mattered. Total recovery would be long and hard for Riley, but with the loving support of his family, Glory knew he'd make it.

"So, Doctor," Brody asked after they drank a toast with Ruby's lime sherbert punch. "What do you think of the clinic?"

"It's marvelous. I can't wait to get to work."

"When do you start, sis?" Riley asked.

"First thing in the morning."

"She's chompin' at the bit, boys," Dub put in with a fond look at his daughter. "I wanted her to take it easy for a few days, but she wouldn't have any of that."

"Hey, I've been waiting a lot of years for this," Glory protested. "Now that I have my license, I plan to use it." Looking pointedly at Ross, she added, "If you don't use something, you lose it."

Ross glanced away, refusing to meet her eyes. He'd seemed uncomfortable during the meal, and Glory wondered if it was her presence that made him so. She could only hope.

"How's it feel to have a dream come true?" Brody teased.

Glory noticed that he squeezed the hand of his own dream come true. "It feels darn good. Everyone should try it."

Again she glanced meaningfully in Ross's direction, but he seemed more interested in his pecan pie than in her. He hadn't said much during supper, and she could only wonder what he might be thinking. As usual, his impassive exterior didn't reflect the internal workings of his mind.

The family laughed and ate and joked and almost obeyed Ruby's strictures against talking business at the table. When the men could wait no longer for horse talk, Glory helped her mother and Noelle clear the table. In half an hour, the women had the dishwasher humming and the old-fashioned kitchen put to rights.

Just as Glory was covering the last of the leftovers, Ross stuck his head in the door. "Thanks for the supper, Ruby. As usual it was delicious and I ate way too much."

Ruby looked up, dish towel in hand. "Oh, pooh, you're as lean as a desert grasshopper. You're not running off already, are you?"

"I have some work to do," he hedged. Glory glanced up and he saw the wounded look in her eyes, but he didn't single her out for special notice. "I'll see you all in the morning."

While Ruby foisted a plate of plastic-wrapped leftovers off on him, Glory decided he wasn't going to get away that easily. She watched as he plucked his hat and sheepskin jacket off the coatrack by the back door and beat a hasty retreat.

As soon as she could do so without drawing attention to herself, Glory followed him. She crossed the screened-in porch where she'd kissed him for the first time, and the door creaked noisily as she let herself out. She walked through the backyard, the boots she'd slipped into crunching across the frost-killed grass. It was one of those mild winter nights that Oklahoma often experienced at the end of February; all crisp air and star shine, with no traces of wind to rattle the leafless branches on the trees.

She was in familiar territory now and didn't really need the moon to light her way. Overhead, the night sky was shot full of stars as bright and hard as diamond chips, and all around her was the comforting absence of city sounds. There was only the deep, insistent silence of nature caught up in slumber.

Phoenix Farm was located about ten miles south of
Norman, a university town made moderately famous
by the Oklahoma Sooners football team. The breeding station was made up of three hundred and sixty
acres and was a veritable community unto itself.
Everyone who worked on the farm lived on the premises, a policy Brody and Riley had adopted at their
training farm, Cimarron Training Stables. If the hands
didn't live there, they'd never get to spend any time
with their families. Even with close proximity to work,
no one rested much during the busy breeding and
foaling seasons, which ran from January through
May.

Top hands and their families had their own homes,
provided in part as recompense for the long hours they
put in. Dub had a number of mobile homes set up on
permanent foundations in which the single men
bunked up two or three to a trailer.

Glory stuffed her gloveless hands into the deep
pockets of her down jacket and glanced across the
road. There weren't any lights on in the house Ross
had occupied since becoming manager, so she headed
for the barns. It was just like him to find more comfort in the company of horses than in that of people.

The heavy barn door swung open on well-oiled
hinges, and she stepped inside, fumbling around for
the light.

"Leave it off, Brat," a soft voice told her.

Leaving the door open to the moonlight, she saw
Ross reclined on a stack of hay bales just inside the
door. His shoulders were propped against the barn
wall, his long jean-clad legs stretched out in front, his
booted ankles crossed. His gray felt cowboy hat was
pulled down, and his woolly coat collar was turned up.

"I thought I'd find you here. I came out to see if I could help you with some of that work you had to hurry back to," she said lightly to let him know she'd seen through his fib.

He twirled a long straw between his thumb and forefinger. "Thanks, but I think I can handle it."

Glory sat down beside him as if he'd invited her. "You didn't have much to say tonight."

"Nope."

"Normally, when two people meet again after so many years they have a lot of catching up to do."

"Is that a fact?"

Glory folded her arms across her chest and leaned back against the wall beside him, her down-covered shoulder rubbing his suede-covered one. "Yep," she clipped in imitation of his own taciturn answers.

"Is that all?"

"Nope. I'm going to sit right here until you talk to me." She wiggled around on the prickly hay until she found a comfortable spot.

"About what?"

She turned around and punched him playfully on the arm. "About the price of pork futures, dadgummit. Anything!"

"Okay. Talk away."

This was getting her nowhere. Maybe if she asked questions, he'd be obligated by good manners to answer them. "Now that I'm home for good, I need to get involved socially. What do you do for fun around here?"

"Define fun."

"Amusement, good times, game playing . . . you know."

"Not really. I never had much time for fun and I don't like playing games," he said honestly.

You could have fooled me, she thought but said instead, "You know what I mean."

"Well," he drawled. "There's a lot of places to go. Norman's a real hotbed of culture—movies, plays, concerts, that sort of thing. If you can't find anything to your liking, try Oklahoma City. You can read all about it in *The Daily Oklahoman*. They devote a whole section of the Sunday paper to that stuff."

"But I want to know what *you* do."

"Why?"

"Because I'm curious."

Ross chuckled. "More likely you're just nosy."

"Come on, Ross." Glory poked him with her elbow. "Do you realize I've known you half my life and I still know virtually nothing about you."

"Not much about me is virtuous," he stalled.

Glory growled in frustration.

"What is it you want to know, Brat?"

"First of all, don't call me 'Brat.' "

"I guess you have outgrown that handle. I'll call you 'Doc' from now on."

"I have a name, Ross. Why can't you just call me 'Glory'?"

He scooted away from her wiggling hip. He couldn't call her "Glory," because he needed the emotional distance a nickname provided. He didn't trust himself around Glory, the woman. He was safer with Glory, the brat. Or Glory, the doc. He answered her first question and ignored the last. "What do you want to know?"

"Why haven't you ever gotten married?"

He gave her one of his famous it's-none-of-your-damned-business looks.

"Okay, so you don't want to answer that one. Let's start with something a little less threatening. Where are you from?"

"Texas, you know that."

She rolled her eyes. "That certainly narrows it down. Texas is only the second largest state in the union."

"Pointblank, Texas."

"Pointblank?" she asked curiously. "Really?"

"Really."

She shrugged. "The name just about says it all, huh?"

"Pretty much. It's a small town east of Huntsville."

"Is that where you ran off to on the few weekends I came home from school?"

"I haven't been back there since I left thirteen years ago. And just for the record, I didn't *run off* anywhere."

"Where did you go, then?"

He stole a sidelong glance at her and scowled. "You're wasted on the horse doctoring business. You should have been a lawyer or a police detective."

She grabbed a handful of his coat front and assumed a TV-tough-guy attitude. "I asked you where you went, buddy, and I expect an answer."

He laughed to cover the shock of her touch. "I went here and there." In truth, he'd spent most of those long weekends helping out at Brody and Riley's spread.

"You never used to go away," she reminded him.

"No, I didn't. There was never any place I'd rather be than here."

"Aha! Then there must have been a woman behind those 'here and there' trips."

She was a *girl* at the time, he thought. "I guess you could say that."

His answer did a lot to spoil her happy mood. "Now that I'm back, will you be going away a lot?"

Ross had entertained the idea of turning up at Cimarron this weekend, but that was out of the question now. Brody and Riley had mentioned at supper that they were leaving for the races in Hot Springs this week. "No, I'll be hanging around."

"Does that mean it's over between you?"

"Is what over between who?"

"Your romance with your lady friend." Obviously Ruby and Dub weren't the area-wide news agency she'd thought they were.

Ross hadn't bothered to correct Glory's assumption that a woman was behind his reluctance to talk to her, because in a way, one was. If he answered her question with a yes, he'd be lying and if he said no, she might think there was someone else. For some reason he couldn't allow that. He shrugged. "You've had your twenty questions, now it's my turn."

"Hardly twenty. But be my guest. Unlike yours, my life's an open book. I have nothing to hide."

He flinched at how closely she'd come to the truth. "Did you meet any interesting men in California?"

"Some." Two could play at his monosyllabic game, she decided.

"You date a lot?"

"A little."

"Any of them smart enough to propose?"

"A few."

"How come *you're* still single?"

"Because none of them met my requirements," she said softly. None of them could compare to you, dummy. She eased closer.

"I take it you've set certain standards for your future husband?" Ross inched away.

"Oh, definitely." She smiled in the semidarkness. If he scooted any farther away, he was going to fall on his butt.

"Such as?"

"Do you really want to know, or are you just making conversation?"

He turned to her and tipped back his hat, and for the first time she could see his face clearly in the moonlight. "I want to know. If you want to tell me."

"First, I think he should be a few years older than me."

Rose grinned. "The inexperienced need not apply, huh?"

She smiled back. "Somebody needs to know what they're doing."

"What do you want him experienced at?"

"Oh . . . life's little mysteries."

He glanced away. "What else?"

"Any man I married would have to love horses."

"Stands to reason."

"And children," she put in.

Yeah, he could see it all now. Dub and Ruby beaming over the grandkids. But what Ross couldn't see was some stranger in the family picture. "What else would you want from this lover of horses and children?"

"He would have to be dependable, loyal and honorable."

Loyal and dependable he could handle. But what was honorable about the secrets he'd kept from her all these years? Nothing. Ross pretended a nonchalance he didn't feel. "So you want a dependable old child-loving horseman. Sounds like you want a guy just like the guy that married dear old mom." She laughed at that, and the tinkling sound of it made Ross happier than he'd been in a blue moon.

"You know what the psychologists say," she teased. "Women always marry men just like their fathers and men marry women like their mothers."

"Not me," he said vehemently. Too vehemently.

Glory looked at him sharply, the laughter dying on her lips. There was more bitterness contained in those two small words than she would have thought possible. This was as close as he'd ever come to mentioning his family, so she did a little gentle prodding. "Tell me about your parents."

"There's not much to tell, I only had one. My mother was sixteen when I was born. She was more interested in having a good time than in taking care of me." He laughed, but it was too hollow to hold amusement. "According to today's standards, I guess you could say her child-rearing skills were inadequate."

Glory felt a sudden rush of emotion for the little boy Ross had been. Thinking of the reliable nurturing of her own parents, she wondered what it must have been like for him to have been raised by a girl who was still a child herself. "What happened to her?"

"She died," he said softly. "Let's talk about something else."

Glory knew better than to press and changed the subject. Before he could move away, she trailed a finger over his mustache. She leaned closer, her lips nearly touching his. "You know, I might like my future husband to have a mustache. But since I've never been kissed by a man with one, I'm not sure I'd like it. Why don't you help me decide?"

"You kissed me today," he pointed out.

"That was nothing but a peck. It didn't last long enough to constitute a real test."

Ross didn't like the direction this conversation was taking, it was too reminiscent of that night on the porch. "You don't know what you're talking about."

"Why do you always push me away when I try to get close to you?"

"It's a dirty job, but somebody has to do it," he mumbled.

"Why?"

"It's just necessary. Trust me."

"If I do, will you help me with my survey?"

Ross couldn't help smiling. "How can I help?"

"Well, just for experimentation's sake, would you agree to be a volunteer subject in the mustache test?"

"I don't know. What would I have to do?"

"Not much." Her fingers riffled the luxurious growth and caressed his lips. "Just kiss me," she breathed.

For once, Ross couldn't think about it, couldn't weigh the pros and cons, couldn't even consider the consequences. With a hoarse moan, he went with his gut reaction.

He pulled her to him with fierce urgency, and when their lips met she kissed him back with a hunger he hadn't expected, an intensity he was unprepared for. It was a caress for his battered soul to melt into, a kiss to remember. Her mouth tantalized, and he drank hungrily of her sweetness.

His lips burned Glory's with their fire, and she pressed against him, transported on a roiling cloud of desire. Her senses gathered into a swelling tide that rushed and ebbed as his trembling hands sought the zipper of her coat. It parted with a harsh screak that seemed to echo loudly in the quiet barn.

Nearby a horse whickered and another stamped a hoof against the floor. Ross opened her jacket and his lips trailed down her throat. Glory shivered with delight and desire.

"Cold?" he whispered.

"Not with you here to keep me warm." She worked the heavy buttons on his sheepskin coat and then slipped her arms around him. She needed nearness, she needed to touch him. It had been so long and she'd been waiting. "Hold me, Ross."

Her hopes spiraled at his eager response, and she sighed against his neck. Gently he nibbled his way across her jaw to her earlobe and back again, finally possessing her lips with a tender yet demanding mastery. His tongue traced, explored, devoured the fullness of her lips and sent waves of need racing to nerve centers that were now on full alert.

When he tore his lips away, Glory tightened her arms around him. "Oh, Ross."

It was the way she called his name and the way she rested her forehead on his chest that nearly undid him. He wanted to keep her close. To take her for his own, to protect her, to love her. He'd wanted it since she was seventeen.

He held her tightly against him, locked in the clinging circle of her arms. Looking down at the crown of her head, he dropped soft kisses there and smelled the sweet herbal scent of her hair. Though tall, Glory's body was dainty and utterly feminine, and he yearned to peel away the rest of her clothes, to see the color and taste the texture of her skin. To experience her completely.

He wanted to nuzzle her ear with his nose, touch the diamond studs in her earlobe with his lips, taste her silky softness against his tongue. But it was wrong to want such things when they could never be. Just holding her like this was torture.

He brought his hands up and removed hers from around his neck, but was unable to move away from her. "We have to stop," he said without conviction.

"Why? I don't understand."

Ross zipped up her coat to give his suddenly idle hands something useful to do. "I'm sorry, Doc. I shouldn't have let you conduct that little experiment." He got up and walked over to one of the stalls before he was tempted to pull her back into his arms.

Glory followed him. "Don't you dare say you're sorry," she said, all the hurt and anger she felt underscoring her words. Without Ross's warmth it was cold in the barn, and she shoved her hands deep into her pockets. "That was the most tender and sensual kiss I've ever had, so don't ruin it by apologizing for it."

Ross turned and rested his elbows on the wooden gate. A long-legged quarter horse stepped up and nudged him. He patted the sleek head before responding. "Then you can't be very experienced."

"I haven't exactly lived in a plastic bubble the last few years. I've been kissed a time or two."

It took Ross a long time to digest that bit of unpalatable information. He shrugged. "It's only right that a beautiful woman like you be kissed. Just not by me."

Glory turned to him. "At the risk of sounding bold, which you've always accused me of being, just why not?"

"Because there can never be anything between us."

"That's not good enough, Ross. Try again."

"Because you're champagne and I'm beer."

"Oh, pooh, is that all?" she scoffed. "I think it's only fair to warn you, Cocklebur, I've developed quite a fondness for beer over the years."

"Just back off, Doc. For both our sakes. There's more to it than you know."

"Then tell me," she demanded.

His tortured eyes eyes gazed intently into hers before he turned away. "I can't."

"The last time we had this conversation, you broke my heart by shooing me into the house like some kid who'd missed curfew. I'm not a kid anymore and I won't be gotten rid of so easily this time. Like it or not, you'll have to talk to me."

"There's nothing to discuss. Go on back to the house before somebody misses you. You want Brody or Riley to come out here and find you necking with one of the hands?"

Glory suddenly did something she hadn't done for years and wouldn't have done now if she hadn't been completely frustrated. She stamped her foot. "Is that how you think of yourself? As one of the hands?"

She didn't know what had happened to Ross to give him such a low opinion of himself. Everyone he met liked and respected him. Her brothers deferred to his knowledge of horses, and her parents thought he'd hung the moon. She knew Ross valued their opinions. What she didn't know was why he was so hard on himself.

"Because that's what I am, Doc. You'll always be Dub's Little Princess, and I'll always be the hired help from nowhere."

"I don't care about that."

"Well, I do." He grasped her shoulders and turned her face up to his. "I managed to stay out of your way for thirteen years. It wasn't always easy, but I did it. Now that you're back home for good and setting up shop on the premises, there's no way we can avoid daily contact. So it's important for us to draw the line right here and now."

"Don't you like me, Ross?" Glory had dreamed of making a new start with him and didn't understand all his crazy talk about drawing lines.

He adopted a deliberately casual tone. "Of course I like you. You're Dub and Ruby's daughter and I've known you since you were knee-high to a fence post. But all I want to do is like you. Get it, kid?"

"What if I want more than that, Cocklebur?" The question anticipated yet another rejection. Dang it, he was beginning to make a habit of this.

"Get it out of your system, or we won't be able to work together. Just because you had some silly infatuation when you were seventeen doesn't mean you want—or need—more from me now."

She could stand here all night arguing with him, but Glory knew it was hopeless. When Ross's mind latched onto an idea, he clung to it like tar on a summer road. Reasoning wouldn't work and feminine wiles were wasted on him. The conversation was over—for tonight. Without another word, she turned and stalked back to the house.

Ross was both surprised and relieved that Glory hadn't pushed the issue. It wasn't like her to relent so easily. He was glad she hadn't insisted on discussing the matter, because he'd used up his limited store of words and at the moment wasn't capable of saying much of anything.

The urgent kisses, the silent plea in her soft murmurs, the way she'd used his old nickname. It had been too much to bear. Glory always had been able to turn him inside out and rattle the pieces, but he couldn't go on like this much longer. Day in and day out, wanting her and knowing she wanted him, but knowing also that there wasn't a damn thing he could do about it. Somehow he had to make her give up on him.

He thought he'd taken care of all that the first time they'd kissed. He'd lost control then, too, but before it was too late, he'd remembered his promise to Dub. He had sworn to leave Glory alone, but all she had to do was swish by and he dishonored that promise.

It seemed more like nine days than nine years since Glory's going-away party and his subsequent talk with Dub. That long-ago conversation came back to him and it seemed he could still recall every word. Less than an hour after he'd sent a tearful Glory running into the house, Dub had been at his door. "We need to talk, Ross," he'd said.

Gauging the look on his employer's face, Ross had dispensed with amenities. "Look, Dub, I realize this is your ranch and I work for you and all that. But it's been a long evening and I'm not in the mood for chit-chat. So let's cut to the chase."

Flashing his possum-in-the-henhouse grin, Dub had apologized for making him chaperon Glory's party.

Ross had stalked to the refrigerator and pulled out two bottles of beer. "I'd rather be a jackrabbit at a coyote convention than do that again."

Dub had laughed and it had rumbled off the walls. "In that case, I'll just say what I gotta say."

Ross stared at the brown beer bottle. "You don't have to. I messed up. I let you down and I know it."

"Who said anything about messing up?" Dub sipped his brew and tried hard to look innocent.

"You and Ruby are important to me, like family. You gave me a job when no one else would and you gave me a home."

"Hell, boy, we got a big place. We wanted to fill it with kids, but I reckon we got started too late." Dub swallowed hard before going on. "When there weren't any more after Glory, we figured the good Lord was telling us to take in the kids who needed us most. First them two Sawyer scamps and then you."

"But they were little boys at the time. I was a grown man and bad news."

"I told you then, Ross, and I'm telling you now. What's past is past. Every day since you been here, you've proved yourself. I ain't been sorry once."

"I just wanted you to know that I didn't start it tonight."

Dub clutched his heart in mock alarm. "It? Just what 'it' are we talking about here? Not the big *it*, I hope."

Ross was shocked that Dub would kid around about his daughter's virture. "No way. I hardly did anything. And I sure didn't hurt her. She's just a little embarrassed is all."

"Hell, I know all about it. You know Glory, she tells me everything. Why, she talks so much, I've considered hiring her to keep the windmill running. She said she tackled you on Ruby's porch and laid one on you. To hear her tell it, it was your honor that was at stake."

Ross grinned. "Not quite."

"She said you sent her away." Dub gazed at Ross, his brown eyes as full of the devil as Glory's. Then his bushy gray brows drew together in a frown. "What I came here to say is that I admire you for what you did. Knowing how you feel about Glory, that took a lot of character."

"Oh, and just how do I feel about her?"

"You care about her."

"I care about you and Ruby, the horses, the ranch. I suppose it's fair to assume that I care about Glory, too." He didn't even fool himself with his casual attitude. "I'll never touch her again. I know I gave you my word on that before, but this time I mean it. I'd pull out of here before I'd hurt her."

"That's good enough for me." Dub finished off his beer and stood abruptly. "But I ain't askin' for any more promises. I know you got some danged idea that you're too old for Glory. Well, maybe you are right now, but she won't be seventeen forever. You think you ain't good enough, but that's a bigger pile of horse hockey than we shovel out of the stables every day."

Ross looked up at Dub, and some of the pain he was feeling must have been showing on his face, for the old man spoke again. "When you drifted onto the place, you had an attitude on you as ragged as the clothes on your back. You reminded me of a good dog that's been kicked so many times he done forgot why he was good in the first place.

"You were only twenty-two, but from what you told me, I figured you'd already suffered enough for a lifetime. Don't bring more misery on yourself, son."

Some of the barriers had loosened when Dub called him that. He'd never been any man's son, and Ross realized his admiration for the old horseman was mighty close to love. And love was an emotion he couldn't afford.

"I made you a promise and I'll stick by it, Dub."

"All I'm askin' you to do, Ross, is to back off until Glory finishes school. You know how much getting her vet's license means to her. It's all she's wanted since she was twelve years old. Let her gain some experience, get some maturity on her. I love that girl, I dearly do. She's smart, but she's impulsive. She lets her heart rule her head, and she just hasn't been around long enough to make sensible decisions."

"What's that got to do with me?"

"I believe she might make a mistake or two where you're concerned, son. Don't let her do that. Ruby and me spoiled her bad and she needs some more time to grow up. Later, if you're still of a mind..." Dub had slapped his thighs and, with a look that conveyed his embarrassment, had said, "Oh, hell, let's talk about *later* when *later* gets here, whaddaya say?"

"Don't worry, Dub, it'll never happen."

"Yeah, and bears don't poop in the woods." The older man had clapped Ross on the back. "I may be a gambling man—wouldn't be in the horse business if I wasn't—but I sure wouldn't bet money on a long shot like that."

"It's more like a sure thing," Ross replied morosely. He'd known how hard it would be to watch Glory gain that experience Dub was talking about.

"Dang it, boy. Cheer up. The Roberts clan is a stubborn bunch, Glory included. And like my little girl says, it ain't over till it's over."

The subject hadn't come up again during the years Glory had been away, and all things considered, Ross had assumed he wouldn't be welcomed as a son-in-law. Just because she was home and more beautiful than ever was no reason for him to go back on his word. Somehow, he'd have to make Glory realize just how hopeless their situation was.

The way he saw it, there were three ways to do that, and none of them were desirable. He could quit his job and leave, but he owed Dub too much to take the coward's way out. Besides, Phoenix Farm was the only real home he'd ever had. How could he turn his back on the only people who'd ever believed in him?

The second option was even more distasteful. He could tell Glory what she wanted to know. She'd been prodding for the truth earlier with those questions about his parents. Why hadn't he just come out and dumped all the shameful facts on her then?

The answer was easy, even to a man as filled with conflicting emotions as Ross. He couldn't bear for her to think less of him. He'd rather she believed he didn't care than be diminished in her eyes.

The third possibility was the most workable, but he wasn't sure he could pull it off. He'd just have to ignore her. Mind over matter. Or maybe he could be so damned unpleasant that she'd finally give up on him in disgust. There was a thought.

The only problem was, Glory Jo Roberts was turning out to be a helluva hard woman to ignore.

# Chapter Three

The rest of the family was gone by the time Glory let herself back into the quiet house. She didn't think Brody or Riley would mind that she'd ducked out of her own homecoming celebration. Now that she was home to stay, they'd have plenty of time for visits.

Her parents, firm believers in the wisdom of "early to bed, early to rise," had already retired. Flicking off the hall light, she walked slowly up the stairs. She was surprised when her mother poked her head out of her room.

"That you, Gloryhoney?"

"It's me."

"Mind if we talk a while?"

Glory held the door and welcomed her mother into her room. Ruby, dressed in a long blue chenille robe and fuzzy slippers, her gray hair wrapped tight in a sleeping net, sat down on the side of the bed. "It sure is good to have you home, baby."

"It's good to be home." Glory sat down beside her and held her hand. "This is what we talked about, all those years ago. Me becoming a vet and coming back here to practice."

"You always were one to figure out what you wanted. Nothing wishy-washy about my Glory," Ruby said proudly.

"I wish I could be so sure about Ross," she admitted.

"Ross?"

"I can't figure him out. I tried to let him know how I feel about him, but he insists on denying the attraction." Attraction? That was a mildly understated way to express the megavolt charge she'd felt when they'd kissed tonight. If there had been a way to translate body shock into amperes, hers would have lit up the whole barn.

"Ross is a hard one to know," Ruby said sagely. "He's had some hurting in his life."

"A woman, do you think?"

Ruby seemed about to say something before she changed her mind. "Just take it slow with Ross," she advised.

"I guess it was foolish to think that once I was home, things would be different between us. He seems determined to maintain a distance I don't understand. For years he put me off with the you're-just-a-kid routine. Well, he sure can't use that anymore."

Ruby laughed and stroked her daughter's hair. "He sure can't."

"I'm not a child with a crush, Mama. I'm no longer a girl finding romance in everything. I've learned that while every story does not necessarily have a happy ending, only those willing to fight for what they want, get it.''

"Don't push too hard, honey. Remember when you were a tiny little girl and you wanted to play with the ducklings? I told you they were too fragile for your little hands.''

"But I didn't listen." Glory remembered. She hadn't been more than three or four years old, but she recalled how much she'd wanted to hug those little balls of down. "I sneaked down to the pond and caught one. I just wanted to love it, but I squeezed it too hard.''

"It wasn't ready for your love," Ruby pointed out.

"And you think Ross isn't ready for it, either?''

"I don't know, baby. I purely don't know.''

Glory wasn't an overly zealous child now. She was a woman and she had mature desires. Where she'd once been naive about her need for Ross, where once the urgings of her body had been a frightening mystery, she now knew exactly what she wanted.

"I want Ross, Mama," she whispered.

Ruby patted her hand before rising, her arthritic old joints creaking. "Then you figure out some way to win him.''

Glory kissed her mother good-night. Easier said than done. So many years had passed, and her predicament was essentially the same as it had always been—fraught with unrequited longing. For some as yet unknown reason Ross was determined to keep her at arm's length, to rebuff every overture she made. His response had been genuine tonight, so why was he being so obstinate?

Was there someone else in his life? If he did love another woman, why was he being so secretive about it? He knew Glory well enough to tell her the truth. Finding out she'd lost Ross to another would be painful and ironic, but it wouldn't be as wretched as thinking the problem was with her.

Surely he didn't think he could simply avoid the issue. After all this time, he should realize that she could be just as determined as he was, that she could match him lick for lick in everything from verbal sparring to an all-out battle of the sexes. He might be stubborn, but he didn't even know what hardheaded was until he'd courted trouble with Glory Roberts.

She undressed and slipped into her nightgown, reliving the security she'd felt in Ross's arms tonight. She wanted to grow old with that feeling, to spend the rest of her life with the only man she had ever loved. But unless she figured out why he was holding back, that would never happen.

There was definitely something Ross wasn't telling her, a secret that stood between them, as unknown and powerful as a force field. If only she could discover what it was, she could change his mind. She could show him how right they were for each other, how wonderful things could be if he'd give them half a chance.

And show him she would. Even if it took forever and a day. Knowing old Cocklebur, it just might take that long. But that was all right—she wasn't going any place.

A cold wind howled in from the north, and bare dark branches scraped against the side of the house. She jumped into the oak four-poster bed and snuggled under the log cabin quilt, recalling other nights spent dreaming in this same bed. For as long as she could remember, she'd thought of Ross before falling asleep.

She laughed at her obsessions and burrowed out a warm, comfortable place under the covers. It wouldn't be as simple to make a place for herself in Ross's stony heart, but then she remembered what Dub had told her when she'd questioned her ability to compete in a male-dominated field: *Nothing worthwhile is ever easy.*

After a forced feeding of Ruby's buckwheat pancakes, Glory was in her office by seven o'clock the next morning, eager to start her first day as a practicing vet. She was dressed in a clean pair of denim coveralls, her long hair tucked up under a cap from a feed store that she pilfered from the hat rack.

She was checking over the equipment and rearranging medicine in the drug cabinet when one of the hands summoned her to the foaling barn where a day-old foal was in acute distress.

Medical kit in hand, she stepped into the stall quietly, murmuring reassurances to the watchful mare. The foal, a spindly-legged little chestnut, was rolling in pain on the straw-covered ground, his head flexed between his forelegs. Glory knelt beside him and palpated his rigid abdomen expertly.

"Morning, Doc," came a deep voice from the stall door.

She glanced up and saw Ross watching her intently. The look in his eyes reminded her of last night and the kisses they'd shared. A momentary thrill quickened her pulse.

"Good morning," she acknowledged before returning her full attention to her patient.

"Meconium colic?"

"Yes." She opened her kit and removed a syringe, filled it with a painkilling drug and injected the foal. Within minutes, he relaxed and ceased rolling. "Want to give me a hand with the stomach tube?" she asked.

Ross held the foal while Glory inserted the rubber tube into its nostril for the administration of laxatives. Once that had been accomplished, they stood outside the stall to make sure the foal recovered and began nursing.

Even though her thoughts were centered on her patient, Glory couldn't help wondering how Ross managed to remain so detached. Maybe she had misread his response last night. Maybe he hadn't been as deeply affected as she had thought.

"What's next on your agenda?" he asked, keeping his eyes on the foal.

"I'm going over to the mare motel to confirm pregnancies. Not a very glamourous job, but you can tag along if you want to."

"No, thanks. I've got work to do. I'll see you when Prescott arrives from Tulsa." Without another word he turned and walked out of the barn.

She didn't encounter him again as she made her rounds through the clean and airy stables, but she ran into Dub, who accompanied her for a while and introduced her to several of the hands. Some of them, especially the older men, seemed reluctant to accept her authority, but she was impressed with their knowledge of horses and hoped that her own skill and dedication would eventually win them over.

During the course of the morning, she confirmed twenty-eight pregnancies among the brood mares, gave routine tetanus and antibiotic injections to several new foals and checked the progress of a number of in-foal mares boarded at the farm by out-of-town owners.

As she and Dub left the foaling barn, she looked around at the impeccably maintained grounds and the facilities that had been designed by one of the state's leading architects of equine housing.

There was a nip in the air, but it held a richly verdant promise that said spring was not far away. The pastures were green with winter wheat, and crocuses bloomed timidly under leafless trees.

"I've missed this place," she said wistfully. She'd been filled with a sense of homecoming since her arrival, but outdoors she was really in her element.

"We've missed you," Dub told her.

"You never doubted this day would come?"

"Never," he confirmed.

"Some of the professors made things tough on the women in their classes. There were times I felt like giving up," she admitted.

"But you didn't."

"No, I'd think about you and Mama and how you always told me I could do anything I wanted. That gave me power. I wasn't about to let a few jugheads steal my dream from me."

"Maybe them making things tough for you was a good thing," he ventured.

"Maybe it was. I know I fought harder for what I wanted. And I have you and Mama to thank for that. You didn't place any limits on me because I was a girl."

"Your mama always accused me of raising you like a boy," Dub said with a grin.

Glory embraced her father in an impulsive hug. "I love you, Daddy."

"I love you, too, honey." Always emotional but reluctant to show it, Dub claimed he got some dust in his eyes and hurried off in the opposite direction.

Glory was heading for her office when she was intercepted by a hand she had not met previously.

"Dr. Roberts," he called to her. "I'm Harvey Tate. Do you have time to look at a mare? She was brought in day before yesterday for breeding and she seems a little lame."

"I have time. Where is she?"

"This way," he directed. When he reached for her heavy medical kit, Glory politely refused. "Didn't mean no disrespect," he said. "I just wanted to help."

"I know, Harvey. But I've been carrying my bag for years."

"I just thought since you were a lady—"

"Think of me as a vet. Not as a woman."

"Sorry. It won't happen again."

Glory smiled at the man who was about forty, slender and fairly attractive in a nonspecific but roguish manner. He seemed quite convinced of his own appeal, however, and kept up a steady stream of chatter as they walked together to the stall containing the injured horse.

After examining the mare, Glory asked, "When did you first notice her limping?"

"Well, she was favoring the leg some when we unloaded her, but we thought she might have kicked the trailer or something. Then yesterday, it was worse."

"Was anyone notified?"

Harvey tugged down his hat. "I meant to tell Ross about it, but it kind of slipped my mind."

Glory was still bent over the horse's hoof, which was marked by a bloody stain. She looked up sternly. "This mare has developed a supperating corn that should have been spotted when she arrived."

"It didn't seem like anything serious to me at the time," Harvey put in uneasily.

"Do you think you're qualified to make a judgment like that?"

"I reckon I've been around a few horses in my day," he said defensively.

"I'm not questioning your experience, Harvey. I am, however, questioning your ability to make medical decisions. What started out as a simple bruise caused by an improperly fitted shoe is now a full-blown infection. I'll give her antibiotics to clear it up and I'll cut away the damaged tissue, but you'll need to get a farrier out here to fit her for new shoes."

"Yes, ma'am," Harvey muttered, all traces of his former amiability gone.

Glory patted the mare's neck gently when she set the hoof down. Remembering what Ross had said yesterday about having to double-check Harvey's work, she added, "In fact, I'll call the farrier myself. I need to acquaint him with the mare's problem."

*"Her,"* Harvey said.

"I beg your pardon?"

"The farrier's a woman. Paula Brady."

She smiled. Times were indeed achanging.

A few hours later, Glory was in her office reviewing the endless paperwork necessary to keep a breeding station in operation. Besides the inventories, complete clinical records for each horse had to be maintained, which showed all vaccinations, treatments, wormings, shoeings and trimmings.

The farm had to keep foal identification certificates, brood mare and stallion passports, breeding certificates, stallion contracts and lease contracts. Forms had to be filled out for every arrival, departure, birth, death.

As ranch manager, it was Ross's duty to keep the records organized, but she would have to work closely with him to make sure everything was up-to-date.

To follow the health status of the mares that came to Phoenix Farms and to maintain an accurate record of preventative medical procedures, clinical records and logs of procedural activities had to be kept in addition to the detailed breeding charts. The health and welfare of over 800 stallions, mares and newborn foals was now her responsibility.

She'd have to get to know each animal in order to understand their individual personalities and idiosyncrasies. She would be on call around the clock and would most likely work twelve or more hours per day. She would also have to make and maintain positive working relationships with the many employees at the farm, as well as the farrier, the drug salesmen, the track officials at Remington Park and, most important, the clients.

Even though she was to be employed full-time at Phoenix, she wanted to make herself known in the community, since she might be called upon in an emergency elsewhere. There were several training stables and breeding farms in the Norman area, many of which did not have resident veterinarians. The managers would be happy to have another doctor available to share the work load.

Dub had explained the growth of the station, as well as the important part she would play, not only here but in the community, and it soon became clear to Glory just how essential her role was. She was excited by the prospect of finally getting to do the work she'd been trained for.

She looked up from her stack of mare charts when she heard Dub, Ross and a client, presumably Mr. Prescott, enter the clinic. She made a few final notations and stepped out to greet them.

"This is my daughter, Dr. Roberts," Dub introduced proudly. "She's the resident vet here now, so she can show you around."

Wade Prescott, a tall man in his early fifties, took a good hard look at her. "So you're Dub's little gal, huh?"

She tried not to be offended by reminding herself that in Okie parlance, she'd be "Dub's little gal" when she was sixty-five years old. "Yes, sir." She extended her hand, but the man didn't take it and she returned it to her side self-consciously. She noticed Ross's studied indifference.

Though her specialty was horses, it only took Glory a moment to diagnose Mr. Prescott's ailment: he was obviously suffering from a disorder that was highly virulent among old-fashioned horsemen. She and her female peers in vet school had called it the you-gotta-be-kidding-how-can-a-woman-be-a-good-horse-doctor syndrome.

Dub, who'd always shown a marked immunity to the disease, was unaware that there might be a problem and excused himself to oversee the unloading of High Flyer. Ross stayed behind, but he didn't say anything, and Glory wondered if he was waiting to see how she handled herself in this sticky situation. Despite the increased number of women vets, it was all too common.

Determined not to let herself get sidetracked by thoughts of Ross or by defending her choice of professions, Glory said matter-of-factly, "If you have your stallion's papers and health voucher, I'd like to look them over before he's brought into the clinic."

"Sure thing, little lady." Prescott waved a manila envelope. When she reached for it, he held fast. "Tell me something."

Uh-oh, here it comes. Glory managed to internalize her groan.

"How come a pretty gal like you decided to be a horse doctor?"

Years of training had taught her the least militant ways to respond to the blatant prejudice she often encountered. Force of will prevented her from reacting to the patronizing tone and the "pretty little gal" description.

"Growing up here on Phoenix Farm," she explained, "I developed a love for animals early. By the time I was twelve, I'd made up my mind to be a vet. I decided to become an equine practitioner because of my affinity with horses and because I wanted to work here."

"Lucky for you your daddy just happened to have a job opening, huh?" he stated snidely.

Ross took a step forward as his famous diplomacy almost failed him. He had to bite his tongue to keep from telling Prescott where to get off. Influential client or not, Ross didn't like the man's tone of voice, but it wasn't his place to butt in.

He glanced at Glory, and her calm, unruffled reaction was a sharp contrast to the spitfire comebacks she'd been famous for in her youth. Only someone who knew her well would recognize that the tensing of her body and clenching of her jaw signaled a fight for control.

"Actually, I turned down three job offers to come back here to practice," she said casually.

"Is that a fact?"

"Yes. One at a racetrack in California, one at a major teaching animal hospital in Colorado and one in Wyoming. A syndicate of horse breeders offered me a five-year contract if I would set up my practice there."

"No kiddin'?" Mr. Prescott's incredulity was still tinged with sarcasm.

"Those who graduate in the top two percent of their classes almost always have a variety of options," she continued conversationally.

"Yeah, maybe you did good in school," he went on, "but how good can you be in the field? There's no way a little old thing like you can handle a stallion weighing over a ton."

"I sincerely doubt anyone, male or female, could handle an animal weighing a ton if it were purely a contest of strength," she pointed out. "With the technological advances we have today, modern equipment and drugs make it just as easy for women to handle large animals as it does their male counterparts. But if it will ease your mind, I have done my share of roping and tying. I've learned never to trust another man's tying."

Prescott appeared to be trying to think of other reasons to disregard her, but reluctantly thrust his horse's papers into her outstretched hands. "Maybe so, but it just isn't a proper job for a woman."

"I understand your concern, Mr. Prescott. Traditionally, mine has been a male-dominated field. But things are changing every day. More women than men have enrolled in vet schools during the past few years," she explained.

"You don't say?" Prescott still regarded her suspiciously.

"In fact, experts have predicted that women will eventually take over the veterinary profession."

"No." The way he drew the word out, it was clear that he didn't quite believe that.

"Equine medicine in particular attracts large numbers of women. The first privately owned equine clinic in the United States was established by a female vet."

"No."

"And Mr. Prescott?"

"Yeah?"

"As long as I have the skill, I can always hire the muscle." She said this last bit with the sweetest smile she could manage.

Prescott eyed her intensely for several seconds and his discomfort showed. "I guess I'll just have to wait and see about that, now won't I?" he asked grudgingly.

She looked over at Ross, who winked lazily. If this had been some kind of test, she must have passed. She conducted Prescott on a brief tour of the facilities, and by the time she was done, the man had had his consciousness raised about female vets, whether he liked it or not.

Later, after she and Ross had attended the first of the artificial insemination procedures involving High Flyer, the horseman was on his way back to Tulsa. He let them know that he still wasn't convinced that his prize animal was in good hands and that he was reserving judgment about Dub's little gal.

"Pompous old poop," Glory muttered when she and Ross stepped into her office for a cup of coffee.

"Don't let that blowhard get to you," Ross advised. "He's all hat and no cattle."

"What do you mean?"

"Prescott likes to throw his weight around and act like he's on top of the world, but I heard he has some financial problems that he hopes High Flyer will solve. I for one was impressed as hell."

"By my facts?"

"By the way you held on to your temper. Maybe you have grown up, after all."

"I've been trying to tell you that."

Ross looked away as he laced his coffee with cream and sugar. There was nothing sexy about the baggy coveralls and funny cap she wore, but he couldn't keep his eyes off her. Watching the exchange with Prescott, he'd come to a startling conclusion. This new, mature Glory was ten times more dangerous than she'd ever been as a teenager.

"I heard you had a run-in with Harvey this morning," he said to cover his discomfort.

"It was hardly that. How did you find out?"

"Harvey told me. He apologized for not noticing the mare's limp sooner. He didn't seem his old surly self and I could almost believe he was sorry. I saw him over in a corner talking to Prescott, thicker than thieves."

"Maybe he was sincere and was trying to smooth Prescott's ruffled feathers."

"Harvey and sincere are two words that will never be used together in the same sentence," Ross said with a laugh. "He's a con man, but as long as I know that, I figure I won't get conned."

"Daddy told me about a horse auction coming up in Guthrie a week from Saturday," she said, to change the subject.

Ross sipped his coffee. "Yeah?"

"I was thinking I might go."

"How come?"

"I want to buy a saddle horse. I miss not being able to ride," she explained.

"If you want to ride, we got plenty of horses around here. Dub's got a whole string of mares."

"I know. But I want my own horse. A paint. I was hoping you might go with me and advise my purchase."

Ross gulped his coffee, tossed his empty styrene cup into the wastebasket and walked to the door. "I don't know why you need me along—you're the horse expert."

Glory debated momentarily on whether she should be totally honest with Ross. If she told him the truth—that she just wanted to be alone with him no matter what the contrived circumstances, what would he do? His darting glance locked with hers for a second, and she guessed the answer. He'd run like a hound-chased jackrabbit.

Forcing a note of indifference into her words, she shrugged and said, "No particular reason, I guess. I just thought you might enjoy the auction. Forget I mentioned it." She sat down at her desk and began shuffling through a stack of papers.

Ross hesitated with one hand on the doorknob and wondered what had really motivated Glory to issue the invitation. She hadn't said a word about that kiss in the barn last night, nor had she acted anything but professional in their dealings today. Maybe she'd thought things over and had given up.

Glory give up? Not very damn likely. Then again, maybe sometime between last night and today she'd decided he wasn't worth the effort. Wasn't that what he'd wanted?

"Maybe I can talk Harvey into going with me," she put in casually.

"Harvey? Why would you want to go with that old buzzard?" Ross demanded.

"Oh, I don't know. He seems like a nice enough guy. Now that I'm home for good, I need to make social contacts. Get out, do things. Harvey would be a good place to start."

*"Harvey,"* he said with forced emphasis, "wouldn't be worth shooting if you needed to unload your gun."

Glory hid her smile. "Why, Ross, you're not jealous, are you?"

"Hell, no, I'm not jealous. It's just that I think you could do a lot better than Harvey Tate, that's all."

She brightened. "I just thought of something."

"What?" he asked suspiciously.

"You could fix me up. You know a lot of men. How about it?"

Ross fumed in silence. Maybe he couldn't follow through with his own instincts where Glory was concerned, but he'd be damned if he'd fix her up with dates. Maybe he'd better go to that auction, after all. If for no other reason than to protect her from opportunistic males.

He opened the door, but before he stepped through it, he said without turning around, "I guess I could go. If you really want me to."

Glory pretended deep personal involvement with her mountain of paperwork. "I wouldn't want to take you away from something more important."

"All right," he said sternly. "I'll go."

"Only if you're sure you can spare the time."

"I'm sure," he almost shouted. He shut the door so hard behind him that the glass rattled.

"Just so you're sure, Cocklebur," Glory told the door with a slow smile. A moment later a laugh bubbled out of her that couldn't be held back any longer.

## Chapter Four

The morning of the horse auction was an unexpected but welcome gift from nature. Clear blue skies and mild temperatures were a special treat for the middle of March in Oklahoma, a state famous for its changeable weather. Dub claimed the day presaged an early spring and a long hot summer, but at the moment Glory wasn't too worried about the future, not even the immediate future. All she was interested in was today.

She made her rounds even earlier than usual on Saturday because no mares were scheduled into the clinic for breeding. Dub had insisted she take the rest of the day off, and considering how hard she'd worked during the week, she felt she'd earned the break. After rounds, she went back to the house to change out of her work clothes. Ross was picking her up at nine-thirty and she didn't want to keep him waiting.

She'd half expected him to try and finagle his way out of going sometime during the past two weeks, but he hadn't and she wasn't about to give him a reason to do so now. She'd tried to tell herself that there was nothing special about today. They were just two old friends setting out to buy a horse.

Sure. That was probably why her stomach had been so tied up in knots that she couldn't even eat breakfast. Ross had done his best to keep their daily contact strictly business, and she hadn't had more than a few minutes alone with him. Minutes they'd spent discussing horses. It was no wonder she was looking forward to having him all to herself for a little while.

Ross pulled up in the Roberts's driveway and honked for Glory. Both the blue pickup truck and the attached horse trailer were emblazoned with the Phoenix Farm logo—a red painted phoenix arising from flames. When the front door flew open a few minutes later, she ran down the porch steps like a carefree teenager.

She looked like one, too, dressed as she was in tight stone-washed jeans and a matching jacket over a pink turtleneck. Her long hair floated around her shoulders in a cloud of curls, and she wore a pair of practical low-heeled cowboy boots. Swinging from a shoulder strap was an eccentric touch that was pure Glory. A tiny little-girl's purse that looked like it had been made from a pair of worn-out blue jeans.

She opened the door and bounced onto the seat beside him. He tensed and his hands tightened on the steering wheel as he tried not to breathe too deeply of her light floral perfume. This was shaping up to be a real bad idea.

"Well, what are you waiting for?" Glory asked breathlessly. "Let's go buy a horse."

"You got your checkbook in there?" He looked askance at the miniature bag.

"Nope. I'm paying in cash. I want to get the registration papers today."

"You seem pretty sure you're going to find a horse you like."

"That's called optimism," she explained with a teasing grin. "Ever heard of it?"

"Once or twice back in the seventies," he said as he eased the truck and trailer onto the county road. "I can't say that I've ever indulged in it personally, though."

"Which brings me to my first question."

Ross depressed the brake and Glory's body snapped against the shoulder harness. "Uh-oh. We're not going to play twenty questions again, are we?"

She laughed and the merry sound of it bounced around the confined space of the pickup cab. She had a wonderful laugh, Ross decided. It was as free and uninhibited as she was.

"No," she said. "I promise."

"Good." Ross resumed driving. It would take more than an hour to reach the sale barn in Guthrie, an historic old town some sixty miles from Norman. During both territorial and early statehood days, Guthrie had been the capital of Oklahoma. In 1910 a local politician, a loyal Democrat, had decided the Republican stronghold was no longer acceptable as a capital, and it was moved in the middle of the night to Oklahoma City.

"How come you're such an old sourpuss all the time?" Glory wanted to know.

Ross sent her a sidelong glance. "Do you think I'm a sourpuss?"

"Don't you?"

"No. I always thought I was kinda serious and pensive."

"You're about as pensive as a sidewinder in molting season," she pointed out.

"At least one thing hasn't changed. You still don't respect your elders."

Ross accused her of being as happy as a skunk in a churn, and Glory's good mood and determination to have fun soon set the tone for the excursion. They talked all the way to Guthrie, or rather Glory did, and by the time they arrived at the auction barn, checked in and received their bidder's numbers, they'd slipped into the easy camaraderie of the past.

They were told they could examine the horses prior to bidding, so they walked around to the stables in back where the consignors displayed their animals for viewing.

Consulting the catalog, Glory saw that there were only a half-dozen paint horses offered: a stallion, two geldings, a mare and two fillies. The stallion and geldings were all high-priced racing stock, and since she had no interest in training her horse for the track, she passed them by. She was interested purely in a high-quality saddle horse for her own riding pleasure.

She wanted a young horse, preferably a two-year-old that she could train herself. That eliminated the mare, a beautiful six-year-old that had failed to distinguish herself on the racetrack. Her choice narrowed down to two, Glory examined each of the fillies carefully.

She tried to concentrate on the horses, but Ross made that difficult by just being there. She couldn't think objectively about equine conformation when such a prime example of masculine perfection was close enough to throw a kiss to. Ross looked particularly handsome today and Glory couldn't quite figure out why.

He was wearing the outfit that had become his uniform over the years: snug jeans, white western shirt, denim jacket, boots, cowboy hat. Nothing at all special about the way he was dressed. But in his case, the earthy, virile whole was definitely greater than the sum of the individual parts.

"Why do you have your heart so set on a paint?" he wanted to know.

"I like their spirit and intelligence." Then with a sly look she added, "And I especially like their flash."

"Since you're basically a show-off, I can see how a downright gaudy horse would appeal to you," he teased.

She ignored the gibe. "Whenever I think of riding, I think of racing horseback across the prairie on a wild spotted horse."

"Are you planning to do a lot of bareback prairie racing?" he asked with a smile.

"No," she hedged. "But it's comforting to know I can if I want to. What do you think of this one?"

Ross walked around the filly in question, whose coloring was a tobiano pattern on a red dun background. He patted its rump. "Good conformation. She's heavily muscled in the hindquarters and her legs look sound." He continued his inspection, but was deliberately nonjudgemental.

Glory shook her head.

"What's wrong with her?" Ross asked.

"Oh, nothing's wrong, she's a beautiful animal. But she's too nervous for my purposes."

Ross, who'd reached the same conclusion despite the fact that the filly was cross tied and unmoving, asked, "What makes you think so?"

Glory smiled up at him. It hadn't been so long ago that she'd been a student telling professors what they already knew in order to demonstrate her knowledge. She still knew the technique. "She keeps her ears constantly pricked forward. A calm, assured horse uses his ears by rotating them toward a sound to show he's interested in what's going on around him. Let's look at the other one."

It was love at first sight when Glory laid eyes on Cherokee Cody, a bonnet-faced overo paint with patches of white on a black body. Her forelegs were white, her back legs black, and she had a high-held white tail. According to the catalog, she was sixteen hands tall, weighed 1250 pounds and was registered with the American Paint Horse Association.

Glory examined the filly, stroked her neck and patted her sides, all the time talking as earnestly to the animal as she would if she had just been reunited with a long-lost friend.

"I take it you've found your horse," Ross said dryly.

"This is the one all right. Let's go in and find a good seat."

The barn itself was a big old facility that was well lit by powerful overhead lights. Folding chairs were set up in double rows with a wide aisle down the middle where the horses for sale could be paraded for prospective buyers. The auctioneer was ensconced on a raised dais where he could easily see the bidders when they held up their numbered cards.

Grooms led horse after horse into the ring. Since this was a stock horse sale, most were quarter horses of every size, age, sex and description. But several Appaloosas were also offered.

Glory admired the uniquely colored horses whose solid bodies were sprinkled with colorful spots over their hips and loins. Descendants of Spanish horses brought to Mexico in the early sixteen hundreds, they had spread northward and were eventually favored by the Nez Percé Indians of the Palouse River country of the northwest—the only tribe to breed their horses selectively. The Nez Percé produced horses that could swiftly chase buffalo and ride fearlessly into battle. The name Appaloosa was derived from the slurring of "a Palouse."

A beautiful palomino stallion was offered next, and he sold for an unheard-of high price. Since palomino foals could only be produced reliably by mating a chestnut and an albino, breeding the horses was an uncertain business. But because of their popularity as show and parade horses, the market for such animals was always good.

It was early afternoon before the lot containing the pintos came up for auction, and Glory strained with barely contained excitement as the first of the six was paraded out. Bidding on the paints was lethargic at best, and she was confident she'd encounter little trouble purchasing Cherokee Cody for a reasonable price.

She reached over and squeezed Ross's hand. She smiled when he looked up, startled at her touch. "Gosh, I love this," she said with an expansive gesture at the proceedings. She was careful to include him. "If I get a bargain, I'll treat you to a late lunch before we go home."

Ross allowed himself to squeeze her hand back before he removed it from her grasp. When she touched him, it had been like a jolt from a cattle prod, but he was enjoying himself. He smiled at the kid-at-Christmas look on her face. Despite the woman she'd become, she still reminded him of the child she'd once been. Her love for horses was so much a part of her that just being in a barn full of them lifted her spirits. "You've got a deal."

The auctioneer opened the bidding at five hundred dollars, which seemed ridiculously low to Glory. She waved her card in the air.

"Now I have five, who'll gimme five-fifty?" the auctioneer chanted in his singsong voice over the loudspeaker. Nodding to another bidder, he continued, "I've got five-fifty, who'll make it six?"

She waved her card again.

Apparently others also thought the bidding modest, because it was soon up to eight hundred dollars. A man wearing a big black Stetson with a rattlesnake band waved his card.

Eight. Eight-fifty. Nine.

Glory gripped Ross's hand nervously. Her purse contained only twelve hundred and fifty dollars, her self-imposed limit on the funds she'd set aside to buy a horse. She'd saved the money during her stay in California by living in the dorm and eating in the school cafeteria, an inestimably depressing experience for anyone over twenty.

Before long, the bidding narrowed down to two people—Glory and the guy in the black hat.

"I've got nine, who'll gimme nine-fifty?" called the auctioneer.

Black Hat waved his bidder's card, and Glory's stomach lurched painfully when she realized the man was determined to have *her* horse, no matter what the cost. He probably possessed a bottomless checkbook instead of a little purse containing all his savings.

She bid a thousand with a sinking heart. Beside her, Ross's look was questioning. "How high are you planning to go?"

"Twelve-fifty, if I have to."

"I have a thousand, who'll gimme ten-fifty?" The auctioneer chanted in the rapid-fire jargon of his trade obviously unaware that it wasn't just any horse at stake here.

Black Hat's bidder card went up again and Glory's spirits went down. Without hesitation, she answered the auctioneer's call for eleven hundred dollars and said a little prayer that the competing bidder would give up. She held her breath and waited for the waving card that would tell her he'd upped the ante yet again.

It didn't come.

"I have eleven, who'll gimme eleven-fifty? Eleven-fifty, eleven-fifty, who'll gimme eleven-fifty?" The auctioneer paused momentarily, surveying the crowd in case someone jumped into the bidding fray at the last moment.

"Going once, going twice. Sold! To number seventy-seven for eleven hundred dollars. You got yourself a horse, young lady." The hammer fell and Cherokee Cody belonged to Glory.

In her excitement, she grabbed Ross and kissed him soundly on the lips. When the crowd around them tittered, he set her aside gently. "This isn't exactly the time or place, Doc," he said stiffly to hide his pulse-pounding reaction.

"Sorry," she murmured, despite the fact that she wasn't the least bit ashamed of her behavior. Could she help it if she had to use every ruse at her disposal to lay one on the reluctant cowboy?

"Come on," she said as she dragged him up out of his chair. "Let's take care of the paperwork and make this transaction official."

Half an hour later, they were in the downtown business district, an area of preserved historical buildings, looking for a restaurant in which to have the lunch Glory had promised Ross. They'd left Cody at the auction barn, with plans to go back and load her into the trailer before heading to Phoenix Farm.

They found a little mom-and-pop café, and when they entered, a welcoming bell tinkled over the door. The aroma of coffee and freshly baked apple pie mingled with the tantalizing smell of the grill, and Glory's stomach rumbled in anticipation of the good food to come.

Two men in cowboy hats sipped coffee at the long counter on the right side of the café. Glory and Ross slipped into one of the vinyl-covered booths on the left. A tiny middle-aged woman wearing a clean white apron over her jeans and western shirt took their order. She assured them that even though it was way past lunchtime, she could still offer them the day's special.

That turned out to be chicken-fried steak with mashed potatoes, cream gravy, green beans, salad and homemade hot rolls. The food came out quickly and as they ate, Ross brought up all the neutral topics he could think of. Topics that were sure to keep things impersonal and remind Glory that just because they were in a restaurant alone, that didn't mean it was a date or anything. Once those were exhausted, they fell to reminiscing.

"Remember Punkin?" Glory asked.

"That swaybacked old nag?"

"Hey, careful how you talk about my very first horse. She was great. I learned to ride on Punkin."

"How old were you?"

"Five. Punkin was already fifteen. I think Daddy reasoned that she wouldn't be able to go fast enough to hurt me."

"Dub cried when she died, you know," Ross told her softly. "He didn't think anyone saw him wiping his eyes, but I knew how much that horse meant to him."

Punkin had finally succumbed to old age, dying peacefully in her sleep, while Glory was away at the university. That long-lived horse had been one of the reasons she'd accepted the grant to do research into the aging processes of animals. The knowledge gained in such studies was essential to the further understanding of human geriatrics.

"I'll never forget the night he called to tell me," she said. "Losing Punkin was like losing a member of the family. Funny, isn't it, how people get so attached to animals?"

"Oh, I don't know," Ross said as he cut off a piece of his steak. "Most of the animals I've known have been a lot more reliable than the people."

"Do you have family anywhere, Ross?"

"Nope." He suddenly became very interested in his mashed potatoes.

"Don't you ever think about having a family of your own?"

"Sometimes," he answered without looking up. He changed the subject by saying, "Dub says you're planning a horse day at the clinic. Tell me about it."

"I've been trying to think of some way to do something for the community, and I had the idea of holding a well-horse day for local kids. If they bring their pet horses to the clinic, it'll be a lot cheaper for them than if I make individual calls. I can check the animals over, file their teeth, give them tetanus and encephalitis shots, that kind of thing."

"That's a good idea," Ross agreed. "A lot of people neglect routine checkups because of the expense."

"And I can offer nutritional advice and teach basic care. I'm committed to preventing future problems, and the more young horse owners know, the easier the vet's job will be."

"It'll also give you a chance to get reacquainted with the people from the neighboring farms and further the cause of women vets at the same time."

"That, too. Who knows? Maybe I'll inspire some little girl to go into the profession."

"When is all this going to happen?"

She chewed her steak thoughtfully. "A couple of Saturdays from now. I need to put ads in the *Norman Transcript*, as well as in some of the small-town papers to publicize it a little. I'm really looking forward to it. I remember how important my horse was to me when I was a child. Horses were my whole life."

"Still are, if today was any indication." Ross realized suddenly how much he'd missed Glory these past couple of weeks. He'd tried to stay out of her way, but because of the nature of their work, that had been impossible. He'd settled for making sure they didn't spend any time alone. But now that they finally were, all he wanted to do was take her in his arms. Right here, right now.

"Maybe." She sipped her iced tea. "But I do have other, more adult interests."

He knew all too well what those interests were. It disturbed him that he still hadn't come to terms with the problem of Glory. Even more distressing was the fact that she was a problem too desirable to solve.

"Will you need any help for the horse clinic?" he asked casually.

"Are you offering?"

"I might be. I was a kid once, too, you know." He forked a bite of gravy-coated steak into his mouth. "Only I didn't have a horse. Didn't even have a dog."

"It's hard to picture you as a small boy," she admitted with a laugh. She wondered all over again about his past and how she could get him to talk about it.

"Probably about as hard as it was for me to picture you as a vet when I first met you. You were just a scabby-kneed little tomboy, but you already had your life's work all picked out."

Ross recalled how impressed he'd been with the young girl's single-minded devotion. Maybe if he'd had such direction in his life at her age, things wouldn't have gone so wrong. If he hadn't made so many mistakes, maybe there would be a chance for him and Glory now.

"I don't know if you've noticed, Ross, but I don't have scabs on my knees anymore." She watched him intently for his reaction, enjoying his discomfort as much as she had enjoyed her lunch.

He nudged his empty plate aside and forked into the apple pie the waitress set down in front of him. He toyed with the flaky crust in an effort to get to the cinnamon-flavored fruit. His embarrassed but gratifying flush told her what she wanted to know—that he'd made it a point to check out her body parts. Many times.

Shortly after two o'clock the next morning, Ruby roused Glory from a sound sleep. "Gloryhoney," she said as she shook her daughter's shoulder. "They need you over at the foaling barn. Rosie Go's having trouble delivering."

Glory had trained herself to wake up immediately. "I'll be there in five minutes," she said as she blinked the sleep from her eyes. She grabbed up her coveralls and zipped them over her sleep shirt. She twisted her hair into a ponytail on the run down the stairs and found her rubber muck boots on the back porch. Hurrying to the clinic for her foaling equipment, she made her deadline with a minute to spare.

A rumpled-looking Ross met her at the door to Rosie's stall. The mare was on her feet, sweating and kicking at her belly. "She started labor half an hour ago and nothing's happened. The foal seems to be lying with its back to one side."

"Have you tried to turn it?" she asked.

"More than once. It's wedged sideways in the pelvic canal and I can't get a grip on the forelegs."

Slipping into sterile rubber gloves, she quickly determined the accuracy of Ross's assessment. "That baby's in there tighter than a tick," she agreed. "I'm going to give her an anesthetic to relieve the tension in the womb, then we'll see what we can do."

Dub stood nearby, watching his daughter intently. When she glanced up, he gave her a smile of encouragement. Most of the time, the mares didn't require the services of a vet to deliver their foals. After all, they'd been doing it for a long time out in the wild without any help from man.

But occasionally something went wrong, as it had for Rosie, and a vet's skills could mean the difference between a live, healthy foal and a dead one. Brood mares were valuable animals, and a lot of expense went into their care and maintenance. A good record of live births was important to a breeding farm's reputation, and it was Dub's and Ross's job to see that the horses got the very best care available.

Glory inserted her hand into the birth passage, lubricated the foal where it contacted with the obstructing bone and finally located the legs. She grasped a slippery foot and, twisting the legs over each other, finally managed to get the head and spine into the proper position for delivery. However, during a contraction, the unborn foal was propelled forward before she could get the legs straightened.

"Great," she muttered as sweat beaded on her forehead.

"What?" Ross asked.

"Now we have a forelegs-bent-at-the-knees presentation. Something tells me this baby doesn't want to come out." Straining almost as hard as the mare, Glory located the foal's foot and bent it forcibly on the fetlock. She tried to lift it over the brim of the pelvis, in hopes of pressing the foal's knee upward and aligning its body properly. As soon as the foot raised into the passage, the leg could then be straightened out with ease.

"Just a few more minutes, girl," Glory soothed the mare. Rosie was trying to be patient, but it took two foaling attendants to hold her steady during the futile manipulations.

"I don't like this," she said in a tight voice after listening to the foal's heartbeat. "The baby's going into distress."

"What's wrong?" Dub asked anxiously.

"It has advanced to the extent that the shoulders have already entered the pelvis. I'll have to use a repeller to push it back into the womb so I can straighten the legs."

The repeller was an instrument with a long straight stem and several branches, two or three inches long, attached to the end. Glory introduced the end with the branches into the mare's womb and placed it firmly against the breast of the foal. When she pushed on the stem of the instrument, the foal was repelled back, and she worked to manipulate the legs into their proper position.

"One more try," she said. "Then I'm doing a cesarean." Just then Glory felt the foal slip into place. Rosie grunted as if in relief and settled herself onto the stall floor, ready at last to deliver.

"Finally," Ross breathed.

"It's clear sailing from here," Glory announced as she stood back to let nature take its course. Ross, Dub and the foaling attendants stepped out of the stall. Within seconds, the baby was born. Glory knew immediately that something was wrong, and when she examined it, she found the foal was not breathing. She was preparing to clear its nostrils to administer artificial respiration when Ross stepped up beside her.

"Don't," he said gently.

"I have to or we'll lose him." Her eyes met Ross's in confusion.

"Let him go. He's defective."

Further examination revealed that the foal had been born with a twisted right rear leg that was malformed and slightly shorter than the others. Such a defect was an impossible handicap for any horse, but a devastating one for a racer. As farm manager, it was Ross's duty to evaluate the foal for confirmation and appearance and make a life-or-death decision regarding the tiny creature who had fought so hard to be born.

"You want me to let him die," she confirmed in a flat voice. When she'd taken the veterinarian's oath, Glory had promised to relieve the suffering of animals, and deep down she knew that this one would only suffer if it lived.

"There's a live-foal guarantee," Dub put in. "The owner wouldn't want us to save a deformed colt."

"Very well." Wearily Glory gathered up her instruments and left the stall. Glancing back, she saw Rosie Go nudging the lifeless foal as though prompting it to get up and nurse. The attendants removed the body before the mare got too upset.

Sensing Glory's distress and wanting desperately to comfort her, Ross walked back to the clinic with her. He didn't know what to do or say, so he stood quietly near the door. She went about the task of preparing the instruments for the autoclave and sterilization.

Glory worked mechanically and tried to reconcile her emotional love for horses with the professional detachment her job required. "I hate to lose them," she said at last, hoping Ross would understand her conflict.

"I know." He crossed the clinic and stood beside her, his hands stuffed deep in his pockets. "There was nothing you could do. Even if it had been an easy birth, the foal would have had to be destroyed."

"I know that."

"We'll breed Rosie Go again, and next year she'll deliver a healthy foal."

"I know."

"You saved the mare. That's the most important thing. She probably would have died trying to give birth without your help."

"I know," she repeated in the same flat tone that held little of Glory's joy for living.

"Are you all right?" he asked softly.

"I'm fine. I'm just sad, that's all."

"Me, too." Wanting only to ease that sadness, he opened his arms to her and she stepped into the warmth and security he offered. He stroked her hair and said nothing, his silent understanding giving her everything she needed. They stood that way for several minutes, finding comfort in just being together.

Although committed to the preservation of life, Glory knew that death was an important part of nature's cycle, a completely natural part. As in the case of Rosie's foal, it was also a way of weeding out inferior stock. As a student, she'd lost patients before and had thought herself inured to the pain and sense of helplessness that was often a part of her work.

"I'm surprised to find out it still hurts," she admitted. "I guess I'll never get used to death, even if I practice for fifty years."

Ross hugged her close, needing the feel of her in his arms as much as he needed air to breathe. His heart was racing in matched cadence to her own, and he wanted this moment to last forever. There was nothing sexual in their contact. It went beyond physical desire to a plane of emotional hunger that was undefinable.

"That's why you're going to be one hell of a vet," Ross whispered against her hair.

## Chapter Five

For the next couple of weeks, Glory was so busy she hardly had time to think about the situation between her and Ross. She rose at dawn, worked all day with the horses and would have forgotten to eat if Ruby hadn't made her daughter's nutrition one of her top priorities.

Now that the days were growing longer, she had time in the early evenings to work with Cody, training the sweet-tempered filly on the lungeline. In the first stages of training, she strived to establish discipline, to teach and demand obedience to verbal commands and to get Cody to use herself and improve her stride. She worked toward the day when the horse would be willing to accept a rider on her back.

Ross frequently dropped by to observe these schooling lessons, often offering words of praise or advice. Proper lungeline technique required a great deal of concentration from Glory, and while she couldn't talk to him, it felt good just to have him near.

At night she visited with her parents and helped them plan their annual party to honor and show appreciation for their many clients. Held at the local country club, the event had become, over the years, something of a social highlight among the horse set.

The early spring Dub predicted held true, and before long the paddocks were full of mares and their romping new foals, many of them gently assisted into the world by the resident vet. One morning Glory was again summoned to the foaling barn to assist an expectant mother.

Toward the end of a relatively easy labor that would have a happy ending, she stroked the young mare's neck and continued to praise her efforts in a low, soothing voice. "It's almost over, Sweet Dream, it's almost over."

"How's she doing?" Ross asked as he came into the stall and knelt beside Glory. He spoke softly and the mare whickered in answer.

"Good, considering it's her first. Her breathing is a bit shallow, but her pulse is steady. I think she's scared, as any new mother would be. The colt is in position and ready." She ran an exploring hand over the mare's extended belly and grinned. "It's time."

When the tiny hooves and wet face of the foal made their appearance, Glory praised Sweet Dream again. "What a good little mother you are."

The foal blinked at Ross as if surprised, and he laughed delightedly. "It's a filly, and she's just as beautiful as her mother."

As they left the stall, Sweet Dream rolled upright and gathered her legs beneath her. With one shaky try, the mare succeeded in gaining her feet. She turned her head, pricked her ears at the foal and whinnied softly. A little intimidated by the strange new world, the filly blinked repeatedly at the noise, then rolled back its lip and emitted a squeaky answer.

Caught up in the wonder of it, Ross slipped his arm behind Glory and rested his hand on her hip. It was natural for her to link her arm around his waist. They smiled at each other—a silent sharing of a happy experience—then turned their attention back to mother and daughter.

Straw rustled beneath miniature hooves as the foal made its first attempt to stand on its spindly legs, but they were too long and its head too heavy. When it failed, the mare gave it an encouraging nudge and it tried again.

With a precarious lunge, the wobbly baby stood, its little flag tail swishing the air victoriously. Sweet Dream made low noises in her throat and blew softly, communicating her pride in her baby.

Ross chuckled at the foal's first attempt to walk. Its long, toothpick legs, which at birth were already nearly as long as its dam's, couldn't seem to decide which direction to take, and it stood in place, shivering. Finally, instinct and nudges from its mother guided it to suckle. The foal's head butted, her legs trembled, and her tail continued to swish.

Ross made no move to leave the comfortable position beside Glory where he found so much peace and contentment. "You missed lunch," he pointed out, "so Ruby sent a care package. It's in the clinic."

"Maybe later."

"Aren't you hungry?"

"Not really." Glory rested her head on his shoulder. Something wonderful was happening between them and she was reluctant to break the spell. "I love this season. This is the best part of my job."

Ross nodded agreement. "Come on, Doc," he said leading her into the clinic. "Let's get washed up."

Afterward he pointed to the covered basket by the door. "Ruby gave me strict orders to make sure you eat."

"Thanks, Ross, but I'm really not hungry. I think I'll take a walk instead. Daddy says the ducklings hatched and I want to go down to the pond and see them."

"Ruby will have my hide if you don't eat something."

She tilted her head and studied him intently. He seemed as reluctant to part as she was. "If you'll come with me, I'll take the basket and eat when I get there."

"That sounds like blackmail."

"It is," she replied impishly. "Are you afraid to take a walk with me?"

Ross knew that all he had to do was tell Ruby he'd tried his best to interest Glory in the food and he'd be off the hook. He didn't have to give in to her not-so-subtle maneuvering. But he wanted very much to stay on at Phoenix Farm. If he was to do that, with even a shred of his doubtful sanity intact, he would have to learn to deal with Glory on a permanent basis.

The past few weeks had taught him that he could never ignore her, no matter how hard he tried. He was no match for the yearning that he'd fought—unsuccessfully—for years. In fact, he had finally acknowledged the feelings he had tried so hard to deny. If they weren't love, they were damn close to it.

He'd considered his other option of making himself so unappealing to her that she would reject him. But somehow he just couldn't follow through. He didn't do anything to encourage her interest, but neither could he bring himself to discourage it. Since nothing else had worked, maybe the answer was to actually spend time with her.

Maybe he could, in effect, innoculate himself against the impossible feelings that mocked him. It was scientifically proven that by injecting a person with small dozes of vaccine, immunity against disease could be rendered. As with other afflictions, maybe love could be guarded against. Wasn't that the theory behind the old saying about familiarity breeding contempt?

Ross nearly laughed aloud at the preposterous notion and imagined a clinic full of hard cases like himself seeking protection against tenderness. Ridiculous. The only thing that worked was to shun emotion.

"Will you come for a walk with me?" Glory asked tentatively. He'd been quiet for so long, she'd become worried. "It's warm and sunny, a beautiful spring day."

"Okay," he capitulated. "We'll walk down by the pond, then you'll eat."

Glory couldn't believe Ross had accepted her proposition. "Why are you so worried about whether or not I have lunch?" she asked as they walked side by side down the path.

"I saw your mama pack the basket, and I happen to know those fried pies in there are apricot. They absolutely melt in your mouth."

Glory laughed at his sheepish grin. "So you do have ulterior motives after all. And here I thought it was my company you wanted."

He wanted that. And more. "The way to a man's heart and all that, you know?"

Sunlight glittered on the surface of the pond, and a gentle breeze created miniature waves that lapped noisily on the bank. Dub had stocked the pond with catfish and bass years ago. Since he wasn't the world's greatest fisherman despite his zeal and hand-tied flies, some of the older fish were practically monsters. They glided along, just under the surface, as if they hadn't the slightest fear of being caught.

Meadowlarks called in the new green grass, and cattails rustled in the breeze. Across the pond a big white duck was guiding her trailing ducklings into the water. The mother quacked and scolded and the babies paddled furiously. From a distance they looked like so many fuzzy balls of yellow cotton.

Glory took the cover from the basket and spread it on the ground under an oak whose branches were heavy and red with buds. Ross sat across from her. Unwrapping a cold roast beef sandwich, she asked if he'd had lunch.

He propped himself against the tree trunk and spread his long legs out before him. Patting his lean abdomen, he said, "I never miss a meal if I can help it."

"It certainly doesn't show," she remarked before taking a bite of the sandwich.

Ross watched Glory's white teeth sink into the bread. When she looked up and saw him gazing at her, she smiled. Tapping his own upper lip, he told her,

"You have a little dab of mayonnaise on your lip, right here."

Glory licked one side then the other. "Did I get it?"

He watched, mesmerized, as Glory's tongue flitted out to swipe once more across her mouth. Her soft pink lips were full and generous and tempting. He knew they'd be warm and moist beneath his own, as he was well acquainted with those lips and that tongue. But not as familiar as he wanted to be.

"Ross?" Glory squeaked, uncomfortable under his scrutiny.

"Hmm?"

"Did I get it?" she asked again.

"What?"

"The mayonnaise," she reminded him. "Is it still there?"

"No, no, it's all gone." Embarrassed that he'd been caught staring, Ross turned to gaze at the ducks in the water. He wondered just how much togetherness he would have to endure before he built up even a smidgen of immunity to her. The change of scenery did no good. Even though he wasn't looking at her, he kept picturing her in his mind. In his arms. Soft and pliant and giving. Inviting him to share...

"Do you want some?" her voice cut into his reverie.

Ross jerked and turned his attention back to Glory. Frowning, he asked, "Some?"

Glory's grin widened slowly, knowingly, as it dawned on her that he was thinking sensual thoughts. She leaned over and swept one of her mother's famous desserts under his nose. "Pie, Ross. Pie."

"Sure. You just caught me daydreaming, that's all." Noting the empty sandwich wrapper, he pointed out,

"For a gal who wasn't interested in food, you sure wolfed down that sandwich in a hurry."

"I guess I was hungrier than I thought." Her mother had packed three small pies in the basket, and Glory gave two of them to Ross.

After eating them, he lay down on his back and propped his hat over his face. Maybe if he couldn't see her, he reasoned, he wouldn't feel so hot and bothered. "If I fall asleep, wake me up in fifteen minutes."

Glory stretched out beside him. "What happens if I fall asleep, too?"

He removed his hat from his face and studied her for a moment. "I'll leave your lazy hide down here."

She giggled. "So who's gonna wake up your lazy hide?"

He put on his Stetson and leaned on his elbows. "Take your snooze, Doc. You were up working long before the sun was up this morning."

"You wouldn't know that unless you were up and about even earlier."

"Guilty," he confessed. "Harvey's sloughing off has cost me my beauty sleep lately. I've given him fair warning, and it looks like I'll have to let him go if he fouls up again."

"I'm glad he's your problem and not mine. However, my beauty sleep was freely given." Glory rolled over onto her stomach and propped her chin in her palms. Their long bodies nearly touched. "I jus' love birthin' babies, Mr. Rhett," she drawled in a less than perfect imitation of Scarlett's errant maid. "I can hardly wait to have a whole passel of my own."

"You've seen some pretty difficult births around here. Seems you wouldn't be so all-fired anxious to go through that yourself."

"Oh, pooh, what's a little pain compared to the miracle of life and love." She looked at him. "Don't you want children, Ross?"

He looked away from her so she couldn't read any wistful traces that might show through against his will. Lately he'd been thinking a lot about things he shouldn't be thinking. Glory was off-limits. And since he doubted he'd ever meet another woman he could love, children were out of the question. He tried to make his tone light when he finally answered.

"Years in the horse breeding business have taught me the importance of bloodlines. Personally, I don't think I've got the genes for it"

"Horse hockey. You fill out a pair of jeans better than any man I know," she teased boldly.

Ross chuckled and tugged his hat down. "Someday that sassy tongue is going to get you in a heap of trouble, Doc. If you say that to the wrong man, you're liable to wind up—"

"What? Married and pregnant? God, I hope so."

"Or worse. Take Larry Dale Toliver for instance. Last I heard he had a total of five children and almost as many wives."

Glory giggled. "I know. And I always thought he was so god-awful green."

"So you did keep tabs on him."

"Mama and Daddy kept me well supplied with local gossip," she informed him. "But he did call me last night."

Ross stiffened. "Is that so?"

"He wanted to know if I needed an escort for the party. Seems he's currently between wives."

Despite the warm sunshine, Ross felt suddenly chilled. Glory was a beautiful woman, and it was only a matter of time before the men around here—men who had no secrets to hide—took a serious interest in her. Once she gave up on him, she was sure to find someone else. He wasn't sure he wanted to be around when that happened. "I didn't know he was invited."

"He isn't, but he kindly offered to escort me."

"What did you tell him?" he asked casually enough not to betray his burning interest in her answer.

"I told him I was going with you," she said as she watched for his reaction.

He sat up. "Me?"

"Well," she explained. "I didn't want to go with Larry Dale, and I knew you'd be there since you're the one who does most of the wheeling and dealing with the clients."

"If you didn't want to go with him, you should have told him so instead of making up a story."

"It's no big deal. Mama, Daddy, you and I will be arriving and leaving together anyway. I don't see any harm in letting Larry Dale think I'm unavailable."

Ross stood up and moved to the edge of the pond, his back to her. "How do you know I don't already have a date?" he argued.

A shiver of panic swept through her. She hadn't thought of that. She got to her feet and sidled up behind him. "Do you?"

Ross kept his back to her and watched the ducks swimming close to the bank. "No, but that's not the point."

"I'm glad you don't have a date, Ross. I would have hated to make a scene in front of so many important people by scratching the woman's eyes out." Glory stepped closer, needing to hold him but settling for the feel of her palm on his back.

Ross sighed his frustration and shook off her hand as he turned to face her. "You've got to stop this," he said hoarsely. "You're making me crazy."

"You're making me crazy, too, Cocklebur." She leaned into his chest, relishing the instant response that always leaped from his body to hers. "You know what's going to happen, don't you?"

"What?" he asked in a husky tone, curious in spite of the voice of reason that warned him not to ask.

"We're going to get together. Somehow, some-day." She paused for effect and looked wistfully into his eyes. "You're going to admit that you love me back and we're going to end up together. Forever."

"No."

"Yes. We're going to make love, Ross—"

"For God's sake, would you just stop it!" He took a step backward. "That will never happen, so just get it out of your mind."

"Oh, yes, it will." Glory took a firm step forward and brushed up against him, intending to wrap her arms around him. But Ross moved back quickly. Too quickly. Suddenly he lost his footing, and his arms windmilled in the air for a moment before he tumbled backward and splashed into the pond. The mother duck took offense at the intruder, and her angry quacks spiked through the air.

"Now look what you've done." He slapped the water, then retrieved his wet hat floating nearby. He plopped it back onto his head, and, dripping with water cold enough to take his breath away, he lumbered to his feet and stalked to the bank.

Glory clapped her hand over her mouth to stifle her laughter. "I'm sorry," she croaked.

"Sure you are," he ground out. "I hope you don't mind carrying your own damned basket home, Brat, because I sure as hell don't feel very obliging right now." With that he took off in the direction of his house, squishing every step of the way.

"Oh, Ross?" she called after him, still trying not to laugh.

He stopped but didn't turn to face her. "Now what?"

"Be sure to change out of those wet clothes right away or you might catch a cold. It's way too early in the year for swimming."

Glory didn't see Ross again until dinner that night, and he had very little to say to anyone, sneezing as he did through most of the meal. He failed to show up for breakfast the next morning, and Dub announced that he'd ordered him to stay in bed for the day because of a serious case of the sniffles. "Strange thing, too," he commented. "In all the years Ross has been here, he's never been sick a day I know of."

"What did you have to do?" Glory asked. "Tie him in bed?" She smiled secretly at the prospect.

"Almost," Dub acknowledged with a laugh. "I threatened to dock his pay if he showed up. I don't want him spreading his blasted germs around."

At noon Ruby insisted Glory take Ross some homemade soup and other cold remedies that she packed in a large carton. It also contained a jar of chest rub, a heating pad and a big box of tissues.

"And don't leave until he eats every bit of that soup. Darn fool don't know how to take care of himself," she muttered.

Because her hands were full, Glory kicked on Ross's door a few minutes later and waited. When she got no answer, she kicked again. And again.

"Stop that infernal racket," he grumbled when he opened the door, wearing nothing but a scowl and tight-fitting jeans.

Glory shifted the box she carried, shoved past him into the living room and set it on the coffee table. Then she turned to look him over critically. "You look awful, Ross."

"I don't need a veterinarian to tell me that," he said petulantly. His eyes were itchy and watery, his nose swollen and red, and he felt feverish.

"Why not? Will Rogers once said that if he ever got sick, he was going to a vet."

"How come?"

"Because you don't have to tell a vet what's wrong with you."

Ross rolled his eyes at her attempt at humor. "Very funny."

"You really should have on a shirt," she scolded him gently. "You could catch pneumonia running around half-naked."

Ross slumped in a chair and said in a sarcastic tone, "I wasn't expecting company."

"Mama sent me. She's worried about you. We all were."

"I told Dub I was just a little under the weather, I'll be fine. It's probably some twenty-four-hour bug."

"You should be in bed," she admonished.

"That's where I was until you started banging down my front door," he said waspishly.

"Come on," she ordered briskly. "I'll help you into bed."

"That's what you've been trying to do ever since you came home," he accused, his words muffled by the dish towel he held to his nose. "Despite my weakened condition, it still won't work."

"Trust me, you're perfectly safe today. I don't want to get sick." She pulled him from the chair and pushed him in the direction of the bedroom.

She frowned when she saw the bed. The sheets were rumpled and the covers were in a tangled heap on the floor. She searched through the linen closet until she found fresh sheets and remade the bed. Folding the blanket and laying it on a chair, she ordered, "Now get between those nice clean sheets and see if that doesn't feel better."

"I might need a quilt," he told her. "First I'm hot, then I'm cold again. And I ache all over. My head is stuffed up something awful."

"You sound like the 'before' testimonial in a cold medicine commercial. Give me that towel and I'll bring you some tissues."

Ross knew he sounded like a spoiled child, but that's exactly how he felt. "Tissues irritate my nose. This is much softer." He climbed into the fresh bed and stretched out.

Glory pulled up the sheet and handed him a T-shirt. "Put this on and take off your jeans."

"No."

"Want me to do it for you?"

Ross glared at her but burrowed under the sheet, wiggling until he had the jeans off. Then he pitched them to her. Knowing there was no point arguing, he shrugged into the shirt. "There! Does that make you happy?"

"Not really. I finally get you in a compromising position and you're as sick as a dog. Just my luck."

"Go make someone else miserable, will you?"

"No one else needs me as much as you do." Her tone was serious, but her eyes twinkled.

"Don't you have anything else to do? What with the party Friday night and the horse clinic Saturday, I'd think you'd be too busy to waste time with me." Ross knew part of his petulance stemmed from the fact that he did indeed need her.

"Everything's already arranged. You're stuck with me." She pressed her hand against his forehead. "You're burning up! How long have you had this fever?"

He closed his eyes and sank into the pillows, his head throbbing. "I'm not sure. Give me my blanket," he said, his words slurred. "I'm freezing."

Glory went to the bathroom cabinet and looked around for a thermometer, but couldn't find one. The man didn't even have aspirin. Thank goodness her mother had sent all that stuff. She found the quilt he requested and tucked it snugly around him.

"Is that better?" she asked tenderly.

"Much."

"Why are you so grouchy? I'm just trying to help."

"This is all your fault."

"It is not."

"Is so," he argued weakly. "I'm never sick, but then I don't normally go for unexpected dips in the pond this early in the year."

"I didn't push you into that pond," she reminded him. "You fell in because you're a chicken."

"It isn't nice to kick a man when he's down, Doc."

"I'm sorry," she commiserated. "Are you warm yet?"

Ross sighed audibly. "Not really. Why don't you crawl in here with me?"

"Something tells me you don't really mean that."

"I'm too weak to fight it any longer." He flung his arms out on the bed dramatically. "Take me, I'm yours."

"I think I'll wait until you regain your strength," she said with a wry smile.

"There you go, trying to confuse me again. First you do and then you don't. First you will and then you won't."

"Sounds like great lyrics for a country song to me," she chided.

He closed his eyes and dozed for a few minutes. When he opened them, Glory was the first thing he saw. "You still here?"

"Yep."

"Why?"

"Maybe I like taking care of you." She flounced out of the room and came back a few minutes later carrying a tray.

Ross opened his eyes and said in a feeble voice, "I thought you'd left me."

"I'm not going anywhere until you're feeling better. I brought you some soup. Can you sit up long enough to eat it?"

He shook his head and made a face. "My throat is too sore to swallow."

"How about some hot tea?" she suggested brightly.

Ross shook his head again.

"You've got to take some aspirin for that fever." In deference to his throat, she mashed two tablets in a teaspoon of water and he swallowed the mixture grudgingly. "The tea will take the bad taste from your mouth and warm you up. Drink it."

Ross sipped the tea. "I'm still cold," he complained. "I'm sure I'd be warmer if you'd get in here with me."

"Absolutely not. I refuse to be a part of your fever-induced delirium."

"Is this another trick? Some kind of new ploy? You're trying to wear me down by making me crazy, right?"

"I've never played tricks on you. I'm taking care of you because I love you, Ross, and it hurts me to see you ill." She brushed back the lock of hair that had fallen onto his forehead. "I'm going to rub some ointment on your chest now."

Ross closed his eyes and smiled, but his words were fuzzy and muffled by his improvised handkerchief when he said, "I knew you wouldn't be able to keep your hands off me."

"No," Glory agreed, placing a gentle kiss on his forehead. "I'll never be able to do that."

## Chapter Six

Glory checked in on Ross frequently during the next few hours, and at times she allowed herself to hope that his temporary illness might bring them closer together. He seemed to want her at his side, to look forward to her visits. But he was too stubborn to admit he needed anyone. Even when he did.

His ailment indeed proved to be a virus of the twenty-four-hour variety, and once he was on the mend and his body temperature returned to normal, Ross's attitude toward her also cooled. She was dismissed from nursing duty with an overly polite, if somewhat embarrassed, "Thanks for all you've done."

The next few days passed quickly for Glory, whose work at the clinic occupied much of her time. Preparations for the reception at the country club were in the final stages, and she and Ruby had to make more than one hurried trip into town to consult with caterers.

By the end of the week, Ross had resumed his primary occupation—avoiding her. He found excuses not to eat at the main house with the family, and Glory had no opportunity to ask him about being her official escort for the party. She knew better than to mention the word "date" in his presence.

He volunteered to drive all three Robertses to the party at the Cimarron Country Club, and promptly at six-forty-five on Friday night he knocked on the door. When Glory answered, she found him standing on the threshold, silhouetted against the deep blue evening sky. His crisp white shirt contrasted sharply with the formal black tie at his neck and emphasized his broad-shouldered appeal. His black tux jacket was hooked on two fingers and slung casually over his shoulder. If she'd thought him handsome in blue jeans, it was nothing compared to the sexy hunkiness imparted by the formal attire.

Ross hated to stare, but he couldn't take his eyes off Glory. The bodice of her dress was a black low-cut tank with a dropped waist. The calf-length skirt was made up of three tiers of ruffles in an electric hibiscus print on black. Her shiny hair curled onto her shoulders, and she was as beautiful and alluring as he'd ever seen her. His first impulse was to pull her into his arms and claim her as his own.

Thankfully Ruby and Dub bustled into the hallway before that unlikely thing could happen.

"I declare, I don't believe I've ever seen a more dashing man than Ross, except maybe for Dub here," Ruby gushed in her usual fashion. Her short but stout frame was draped in a voluminous mauve chiffon caftan, and an orchid corsage bloomed on her shoulder.

Dub, who was more at home in jeans, looked uncomfortable in his rented black tuxedo and tugged at his collar. "Mama insisted this dang bow tie and whatchamacalit—"

"Cummerbund," Glory supplied.

"Whatever. Anyhow she wanted them to match her dress."

"You're quite the striking couple," Glory told them.

"Oh, hell," Dub complained. "We look like a couple of geriatric teenagers heading to the prom."

"Oh, pooh, we do not," Ruby said as she herded everyone out the door. "We'd better get a move on, it wouldn't look good if we were late to our own party, now would it?"

Dub helped his wife into the back seat of the family sedan and Ross opened the front door for Glory. Ruby chattered excitedly all the way to the country club and claimed she felt like she *was* going to the prom. Ross drove them to the door and instructed them not to wait for him, but to go on in while he parked the car. Dub had vetoed valet parking since so many of his old cronies had complained about the young men last year.

Nearly an hour passed and Glory still hadn't caught up with Ross. She decided that if he had ducked out without a word to her, he would have some tall explaining to do. Dub had showed her around, introducing her to their clients and other important people in the horse business. Racetrack officials from Remington Park were present, as were a number of quarter horse breeders, owners and trainers. Brody and Noelle danced by her a few times, but they were so preoccupied with each other that they'd had time for little more than a perfunctory hello.

Glory had never thought of Riley the Runaround as the wallflower type, but tonight he'd found refuge from the attentions of unattached females by hiding in a cluster of horsemen talking business. It was disturbing to see him pining like this, but she'd had a chance to discuss the matter with Noelle and had learned that her brother's real problem was a broken heart. According to Noelle, he was still in love with a friend of hers, Darcy Durant.

She scanned the room while trying to attend to the conversation of the darkly handsome man hovering around her like a helicopter looking for the perfect landing spot.

"May I get you a fresh drink, *querida*?"

"This one is fine, Carlos, but thanks anyway." Darling? Ugh. She smiled weakly at the self-centered Latin lover beside her and sipped her ginger ale. The man, Carlos San Rio, was a wealthy Puerto Rican who owned and showed a stable of beautiful Paso Fino horses. He had attached himself to her like a leech the moment they were introduced and as yet showed no sign of letting go. He took advantage of every chance to touch her and "undress her with his eyes" as it was described in novels.

Carlos spoke again, dropping names and lacing his remarks with subtle hints of how rich and important he was, pointing out how nice it was in Saint-Tropez this time of year.

Glory stifled a yawn and allowed her gaze to drift around the crowded room of the Cimarron Country Club in search of Ross. She'd rather be in a barn with him than on the French Riviera with this jerk whose

IQ and personality were roughly those of a raisin. And not even one of the singing, dancing raisins at that.

"The moment you walked in, I say to myself, Carlos—" he smiled to show his perfect white teeth "—you must meet this *señorita* who possesses such *belleza*—that is Spanish for beauty," he explained with another blinding grin.

"You're very kind," she offered. Strains of a slow country ballad filtered in from the ballroom next door, and Glory glanced wistfully in that direction, wondering if Ross was in there dancing and enjoying himself while she was cornered here at the buffet table.

"Do you desire to dance, *querida*?" Carlos asked with a bit too much verbal emphasis on the word desire.

"No, but thanks for asking." Glory shook her head and tuned out the flow of flattery that followed, wishing she could dredge up enough high-school Spanish to tell him to get lost. The next thing she knew, Carlos was offering to take her away from this boring party to his place where they could make their own. Party, that was.

"No," she said tersely. Deciding she'd done her duty in the good manners department, she turned away and finally spotted Ross in the crowd. "Nice meeting you, Carlos, but I must mingle. *Adiós, amigo.*" Sensing the persistent Puerto Rican following her, she strode purposefully toward the group of men insulating Ross, in hopes of losing him.

Nothing was worse, she thought, than a man with a mission. Knowing nothing short of radical surgery would remove him from her side, Glory pulled one of her old college tricks.

She walked right up to Ross and put her arms around his waist, reached up on her tiptoes and kissed his cheek.

"Hi, honey, I thought I'd lost you in the crowd." Turning to her would-be suitor, she said, "Carlos San Rio, meet Ross Forbes." Her lips to Ross's ear, she murmured. "Get me away from this Casanova."

Ross figured out the situation immediately and was grateful that Glory wanted to be rescued. With her arm still around him, he extended his hand and eyed the man warily.

"Señor San Rio." Ross nodded. He wanted to tell the man that Glory was spoken for, but that was impossible. He couldn't afford to let her know just how deeply involved his feelings were, but he wasn't about to let this Latin lover get his claws into her. He screwed his lips into a facsimile of a smile. "Excuse us, gentlemen, but I did promise to dance with the doc."

Glory smiled, hooked her arm in his and said, "And I have it on good authority that Ross Forbes is a man of his word."

Ross kept the cardboard smile in place and, shaking his head, led her away. Instead of dancing when they reached the ballroom, he led her out the French doors onto the terrace. Tulips and narcissus bloomed in the garden beyond, and the warm breeze carried the scent of those early flowers. The rambling brick building with its white columns and wide verandas was part of a magnificent setting. Situated on a rocky bluff, it overlooked a large man-made lake.

Ross and Glory stood near a waist-high brick wall and looked out over the moon-washed water.

"Thanks for the rescue, Ross. Carlos doesn't understand the meaning of the word 'no.' In English or Spanish."

Ross shoved his hands into the pockets of his rented tux so they wouldn't try to touch her against his will. "Maybe you shouldn't wear such sexy dresses. I seem to recall another time when too much sophistication got you in trouble."

His hungry eyes roamed the length of her and, angry at himself for allowing it, he said, "That top is way too low cut and clingy."

"Thanks," she said sweetly. "I'm glad you like it. I picked it out with you in mind."

"You shouldn't have bothered," he grumbled.

She grinned at him. "If we'd been alone, I wouldn't have."

Ross turned away from the beguiling sight of her and looked out at the lake once more. "Cut it out, Doc, you're not fighting fair."

"All's fair in love," she said softly.

"And war," he reminded her.

"Let's not fight." She tentatively touched his arm. "I thought we were going to dance."

Ross turned back, staring down at her. Finally he forced himself to speak. "I think we'd best forget about that."

"You said we were going to dance. Surely you aren't going to go back on your word?"

He rolled his eyes heavenward. When Glory wanted something, she got it or knew the reason why. "All right," he conceded, "one dance and that's it."

He put his left hand on her hip and was about to take her hand in the other, but she placed both arms around his neck and stepped up to him, nestling her cheek against his. Finally he wrapped his arms around her waist and they swayed slowly to the music.

Glory closed her eyes and soared with the feeling of his warm hands on her back as they glided around their own private star-studded ballroom. His heart beat wildly in tempo with hers. They fit together perfectly—in more ways than one—and she meant to prove it to him.

Ross tried every trick in the book to keep from falling into the sensual abyss that threatened him whenever he was this close to Glory. If just dancing with her did these things to his mind and body, what would it be like to actually make love to her?

In an effort to put those thoughts from his mind, he tried to silently recite the multiplication tables. But nothing could dim the pleasure of holding her in his arms. She was so close he could feel the warmth and pliancy of her body. Holding her felt so good, he forgot that he shouldn't enjoy it.

An overwhelming gladness swept over him, and he closed his eyes to savor the sweet feel of her for the length of the dance. The press of her thigh against his, and her fingers as they caressed his neck beneath his hair, was almost more than he could bear.

Needing to see his face, Glory leaned her head back. She smiled at the look of contentment on his features. "Isn't this better than fighting?" she said softly.

Ross smiled back at her, reluctant for the magic to end. For just a little while he wanted to pretend there was no horrible past to keep them apart, no promise to be broken. "Hush, Doc, don't spoil it with words."

She raised her lips as slowly as his descended, and Ross was ill prepared for the shock of wanting heat that spiraled through him as the kiss deepened. Her tongue traced his bottom lip and he crushed her to him.

Glory gave herself freely to the passion that sent her senses whirling. His firm, warm mouth devoured her softness, moving slowly and thoroughly, demanding a response, and she gladly gave it. When his lips seared a path down her neck and her bare shoulders, she felt the soft brush of his mustache on her skin. His hands roamed over her back, caressing her through the soft fabric of her dress.

"I shouldn't be doing this." His voice was raspy with emotion.

Glory held tightly to him. "Don't say that." Her lips touched his cheek. "We were meant for each other. Why can't you understand that?"

Lightly he fingered a loose tendril of hair on her cheek. "It's *you* who doesn't understand."

Glory reclaimed his lips, desperate, demanding.

"I promised Dub this would never happen." Ross grasped her shoulders and wrenched her away from him. "I can't do it."

"Nobody does it better, Ross. Nobody."

"If you ever needed rescuing, you need it now. From me. Go inside and let your daddy take care of you from now on."

"But, Ross—"

"Just go." He turned his back on her and strode across the terrace and into the trees.

She stood there, wondering what she'd done wrong and gazing longingly after him, when she heard her father's voice behind her.

"Glory." Dub put his arm around her shoulders and led her into the ballroom. "I've been looking for you, honey. Thought I'd introduce you to some more of the folks we do business with."

She forced a smile. "Could it wait, Daddy? I don't feel like meeting anyone right now. I need to talk to you about Ross."

"What about?"

"I love him. I always have."

"Well, I reckon that don't surprise me none."

"He's holding back and it's because of something he promised you. Do you disapprove of Ross? For me?"

"Hell, no," he said vehemently. "Truth to tell, I've been wondering when you two would get together."

"I'm beginning to wonder if we ever will. Are you sure you have absolutely no objections?"

"I trust him completely. Ross is a good man, I've never doubted him."

"Then why would you make him promise to stay away from me?"

Dub looked confused for a moment. "Promise? Lordy, honey, that was a long time ago. When you were just a kid. I figured he knew those old rules don't apply now."

"I want you to tell him. Will you?"

"Well, sure thing. If you think it will do any good."

"Thank you, Daddy." Glory hugged her father. "I love him so much. And I know he feels the same way I do, but something is holding him back. Once he realizes it's okay with you, maybe he'll admit it."

Dub patted his daughter's shoulder affectionately. "I can't make him love you back, Glory. But I'll see to it that he knows you two have my blessing."

Ross walked down to the lake and back, thinking about what he should do. Life sure was complicated

sometimes. He considered going to Glory and telling
her the whole truth. But then he thought of the dis-
appointment and distrust he'd see in her eyes and he
couldn't follow through. He couldn't tell her now, after so many years. His silence was as condemning as
his original crime.

He returned to the terrace and watched Dub approach. "I hope you didn't skip out here to sneak a
cigarette, Dub. Because if Ruby asks me, I'll have to
tell her the truth."

The older man chuckled and held out his hands to
show he had nothing to hide. "I really did quit this
time, Ross. I just came out here to talk."

"If it's about Glory, forget it."

"Well, now, I can hardly do that. She's mighty upset." Dub sat down on the low wall. "Nine years ago
I told you we'd talk about this later, and it looks like
later finally got here. We'll talk now."

Ross leaned one hip against the wall. "I'm listening, but nothing you can say will make any difference."

"When you first came to us, Glory was only thirteen and I was concerned about her infatuation with
you. Hell, every hand on the place knew better than to
mess with her, because she was my daughter. But I
could see she took a shine to you right off. All I knew
I had to do was ask you to stay away from her, because I figured I could trust you to keep your word."

"I've done my best, Dub."

"It ain't been easy, has it?" Dub laughed and
clapped him on the back. "I know you've never let me
down, not once. I want you to know that I'm releas-
ing you from that promise as of right now."

"What if I don't want to be released."

"Are you saying you don't care for Glory?" Dub countered.

"I'm telling you something you should already know. I'm not the man for her. She deserves better than me."

"Because of what you did?"

Ross nodded.

"Hell, you were just a scared kid. It was an accident. You paid your debt to society, and you've repaid any debts to me a hundred times over."

"It's not that simple, Dub. I wish it were."

"Maybe not, but what's done is done, and all that never made a bit of difference to me. I got a feeling it won't matter none to Glory, either."

"No, it won't," Ross agreed, "because she won't ever know."

"If I know my daughter, and I do, she'll find out. She means to have you, son, and she'll mow down anything that's got the gall to stand between her and you. If you want, I'll explain things to her, but it'd sit a sight better coming from you."

"I don't want her to know," Ross repeated stubbornly.

Ruby stuck her head out the French door and, spotting Dub and Ross, joined them. "What are you two doing out here?" Without giving them a chance to answer, she gave Dub a quick kiss, saying, "At least you haven't been smoking or I would smell it. You men have been hiding out here long enough. The party's winding down, so we'd better get in there and say goodbye to our guests. I swear, it seems to me y'all would get enough of each other's company without having to slip—"

"We're coming, we're coming," Dub interrupted. "Let's go do our duty, Ross, else this woman's gonna chew off our ears."

Ross laughed and ushered them into the building to say their farewells to what was left of the guests. He managed to put up a good front, but he couldn't get the conversation between him and Dub off his mind. Maybe he should come clean. Suffer the consequences.

Pay for his crime all over again.

As much as it pained him, he knew that in the end Glory would be hurt. No matter how he handled this. But it could hurt more if she found out he was less than the man she thought he was. No, he wouldn't tell her. He'd wanted to discourage her, to demonstrate that there was no future for them. But he wasn't very convincing.

On the way home Dub and Ruby provided a smoke screen of small talk, but Glory and Ross made the trip in silence.

"What the devil's going on in the stallion barn?" Dub asked as they piled out of the car in front of the house. "It's lit up like a Christmas tree."

"You all go on in," Ross said curtly. "I'll handle it, whatever it is."

Glory was at his side in a moment. "I'm coming with you."

"Suit yourself." Ross turned and covered the distance at a trot.

Her three-inch heels kept bogging down in the soft ground, so she stopped to slip them off. By the time she reached the barn, Ross was already inside, his tux jacket hung carelessly on a nail, his bow tie dangling limply at his open collar. He was barking orders to the men, and Glory was struck by the grim look on his face. She'd never seen him so angry.

The stallions were normally kept separated with at least one empty stall between them, but now several were loose, and Ross was helping an equally grim Harvey subdue the frightened animals and return them to their stalls.

The barn was filled with their squeals and whinnies, and High Flyer and another stallion were actually nipping and striking at each other. Several of the less aggressive horses milled around outside their stalls while the hands tried to round them up.

With no regard for her expensive new dress, Glory pitched in and they soon had things under control. She looked at Ross as the last animal was led away. "We make a funny looking pair of wranglers," she said with a dusty grin. "You in your black tie and me in my ruined panty hose."

Ross wasn't really listening. He was fighting down the dark anger that had roiled up inside him when he realized the horses had been placed in jeopardy by someone's carelessness. And he had a pretty good idea just whose carelessness was involved here.

"Harvey!" he called in a voice like quiet thunder. "I want to see you in my office." His tone was still tight but under control when he thanked the rest of the men for their help and sent them off to bed.

Finally he turned to Glory as if he'd just remembered she was there. "Thanks."

He was dismissing her, too. "I thought I'd wait for you so we could talk."

"Not tonight. I've got my hands full." Ross headed toward the clinic and his office.

Glory followed. "When?" she persisted. "When will you ever get around to me?"

He stopped, but didn't turn around. "I don't know, Doc," he said tiredly. "Probably never."

"Go do what you have to do," she said softly. "But I won't go away simply because you ignore me, Ross. How many times do I have to tell you before it sinks into your thick skull? I'm not going to give up." With that she marched back to the house.

"Don't I know it," he muttered to himself as he watched her go, perversely longing to call her back now that he'd sent her away.

When he reached the office Harvey was already there, waiting nervously.

"You were on duty tonight," he said without preamble. "What the hell happened?"

"I ain't too sure, Ross. I reckon I forgot to latch the stable gates after I mucked out tonight."

"You forgot!" Ross smelled the sour odor of cheap whiskey on the older man's breath.

"Hey, it's no big deal. No real harm was done, they didn't get into any extra feed, or get hurt, or nothin'."

"But they could have, Harvey. Bobby said the barn door was open, and several horses might have wandered off if he hadn't come outside to empty his garbage when he did."

"Well, it won't happen again. I swear," Harvey said, his words slightly slurred.

"No," Ross agreed. "It won't happen again. As of right now, you don't work here anymore. You can stay in the trailer with the others for a few days until you find another job, but I won't be able to give you a good reference."

"Aw, man, can't you give me another chance," he whined as he cut his eyes away.

"You've had more than your share and you've used them all up. I've given you the benefit of the doubt before, but tonight you endangered the well-being of the horses. I can't overlook that. I told you the last time, I'd have to let you go if anything else happened because of your negligence."

"To hell with you! You ain't no better than me, Forbes. You might have everybody else fooled, but I know all about you." Harvey's laugh was ugly.

"What do you know?" Ross was sure he'd never seen Harvey before he came to work at Phoenix Farm. He stared at him warily, waiting.

"I been around. I been all over Texas, lived in Austin for a spell about seventeen years ago," Harvey said smugly.

Ross stiffened. "So get to the point."

Harvey sneered. "You don't know me and I never knew you personally. But I sure as hell *remember* you. Your name and picture were in all the newspapers."

"You're still fired." Ross stood up slowly, his hands clenched into fists at his sides. He managed to keep his voice level as he struggled to retain his composure. "Get your things together and clear out of here. Tonight."

"Oh, I'm goin'." Harvey jumped to his feet, clomped to the door and threw it open. "But I wonder how that prissy little gal and her rich daddy are gonna feel when they hear you killed a man."

Ross glared at him, fighting the rage that he'd always feared would overcome him again someday. "If they hear it from you, it better be by telephone, or mail, because if I see you on the premises after to-night, I'll—"

Harvey interrupted the threat with one of his own. "You won't see me, I promise you that. But you'll get your comeuppance, jailbird." He slammed out of the room without giving Ross a chance to react.

Ross slumped into his chair and, propping his elbows on his desk, rested his head in his hands. He'd never doubted that the past would catch up with him sooner or later. That's why he'd been in such agony since Glory came home. He just hadn't expected it to happen like this.

He sat there and Harvey's hateful words screamed over and over in his mind. He'd killed a man.

Killed.

The words left a bitter taste in his mouth, and he knew he could never change what he was, never undo the damage he'd done. No matter how many years he lived as a model citizen, he could never make up for that one terrible moment.

That night had irrevocably changed his life forever. He recalled it in painful disjointed snatches, memories that were like watching an old movie that had been looped wrong. Coming home and finding his mother and her lover in the middle of a fight. The big man hitting her, kicking her when she fell. Cursing her.

He could still hear his mother's screams, her whimpers. Her begging. A powerful rage that slept inside him like a monster had blinded him, and he'd struck back at his mother's attacker. Slammed him into the wall. The horrifying red stain that smeared the wall as the man slid to the floor.

The fury had subsided and he'd knelt by his mother, crying, pleading with her to hold on until help arrived.

Then the sheriff was there, taking him away in handcuffs. They'd only allowed him to see his mother once before she died. The intensive care ward. A once pretty young woman broken and bruised beyond recognition and recovery because she'd wanted a rich man's son to love her. Attached by tubes and wires to the beeping machines that kept her alive. But only until her weary heart finally stopped and she found the peace that had eluded her in life.

A trial that had been more joke than miscarriage of justice. Prison. The whole sordid cliché of a kid who had to grow up fast, fighting to survive. Ross groaned. He couldn't tell Glory, who was everything good and sweet in the world, about that ugly part of his life.

And he couldn't tell her that he'd killed a man in rage. That he woke up from nightmares, drenched in cold sweat. Even after so many years, it still frightened him that he could possess such violence.

It would surely horrify her.

He thought he'd overcome it. He'd worked hard to make certain that nothing like that ever happened again. Because he'd never been sure of his impulses or emotions, he'd fought them, denied them, whipped them into submission. But he was wrong. Tonight he'd been deeply angered by Harvey's irresponsible actions, and he'd had a glimpse of what he could be.

His only option now was to leave.

## *Chapter Seven*

On Saturday Ross began to make plans. He'd spent a sleepless night going over his choices and knew he really didn't have any. Now that the past had finally caught up with him, he really did have to leave Phoenix Farm. With the memory of Harvey's threat playing like a stuck record in his head, he searched out Dub. Ross made it clear they needed privacy to talk, so they walked down by the pond.

It was a crisp spring morning, and the sun rode high in a cloudless sky the color of a robin's egg. The new leaves on the oaks and hickory trees fluttered in the slight breeze, and a blue jay couple scolded noisily in the branches. The duck family was waddling around on the opposite bank, squawking and picking bugs out of the grass.

Ross needed something to do while he figured out how to tell Dub he was leaving, so he picked up a handful of smooth stones and skimmed them over the rippling surface of the pond. He was grateful that Glory was tied up at the clinic, conducting the horse day for the local kids. Telling Dub would be bad enough, but what he had to say would be that much harder if he had to face her, too.

Dub listened solemnly as Ross explained what had happened with Harvey last night. But when he finally got around to his decision to leave, the older man tried to talk him out of it.

"I know I never really said it in so many words, but I always hoped you'd take over here someday. Me and Ruby want to retire as soon as Glory gets settled in good and proper. Buy us a place on the lake and do some fishing." There was a catch in the older man's voice.

"You can still do that. Glory's capable of running the outfit for you. All she needs is a good man to take over my job."

"Don't know who that would be. Got any ideas?"

"Not at the moment." Ross found it difficult to look Dub in the eyes. Why did everything have to be so complicated?

"I'd appreciate it if you could see your way clear to stay until the end of the foaling season and help me find a replacement."

"I'd like to help you out, Dub, but I shouldn't hang around now that I've made up my mind. It'll only prolong the agony."

Dub watched the pebble Ross tossed as it skipped once, twice, three times across the water. He nodded resignedly. "You're right. It's too much to ask when you've got your plans all made and everything."

Ross clenched his jaw and skipped the last stone with a vengeance. Compared to everything Dub had done for him over the years, he wasn't asking much in return. Ross felt selfish for denying his request now. "I don't really have any plans, but I think staying would be a mistake."

"When are you leaving?"

"In a week."

"Do you have another job waiting? With your savvy and experience, I reckon you can work anywhere you want."

"I don't have anything lined up. I have a little money set aside. I may decide to buy me a small place of my own somewhere." But what joy could he take from it without Glory?

Dub brightened. "Hell, if you're looking to buy a spread, why not this one? I'm willing to make you a real good deal on a controlling interest."

Ross fought to hide his emotion. Owning a piece of Phoenix Farm had always been his secret dream. He longed to live out his days on the land that had given his life back to him. This land that had somehow gotten into his blood. "There's nothing I'd like better," he admitted. "But you know I can't stay."

"I don't know any such thing, but I know you. If you're set on it, I reckon I got no choice but to accept your decision. But I sure as hell don't understand it." Dub shook his head sadly and put a fatherly hand on Ross's shoulder. "You can't keep running from the past, son. It's like a shadow. There'll be days it won't show up and some days you won't even think about it. But it's there all the same. You gotta learn to live with it."

"Maybe, but it's my shadow. I can't inflict it on Glory."

"I guess I can't talk you out of this foolishness, but you owe Glory an explanation of some kind. She's gonna pitch a hissy fit for sure."

"I'll tell her. And I'll make it as easy as I can." Ross nodded and his Adam's apple worked around the lump in his throat. How would leaving Glory ever be easy? He extended his hand in a gesture of sincerity.

"We might not get another chance for this much privacy, so I'll say this now and get it over with." Tears filled his eyes as Dub ignored Ross's hand, pulled him into a manly embrace and clapped him soundly on the back. "I'll miss you, son, and I want to know where you wind up. You hear?"

"Yessir, I'll let you know." Ross hugged the old man for a second.

"I want us to keep in touch. You're like a son to me."

Ross's eyes moistened. "No father could ever have done more than you've done for me. Thanks for everything, Dub."

Dub pounded him on the back again, then turned and started down the path. He stopped suddenly and looked back over his shoulder. Somewhat sheepishly he said, "I almost forgot something. Brody and Noelle invited us to dinner at their place tomorrow and they want you to come, too."

"I don't think—"

"Please," Dub entreated. "Do it for me and Ruby."

Ross sighed. The old fox sure knew how to work him. "Okay, I'll go."

As soon as Dub left, Ross slumped down in the shade of an oak tree, wondering how he'd ever get through the next few days. His thoughts were bitter and his spirits sank to an all-time low. He missed everyone and he hadn't even left yet. He would miss the camaraderie of the whole Roberts family, but the thought of leaving Glory caused the most pain.

Ross steeled himself against the ache. He didn't have time to sit around moping about what *might* have been. This was the way things really were. He was leaving and that was that. In the meantime, he had preparations to make, loose ends to tie up. Goodbyes to say.

On Monday he'd call the bank and finalize the financial arrangements he'd already initiated. He didn't have enough money to buy a place like Phoenix Farm, but what he had would give him a new start somewhere.

Where? He didn't know yet, but maybe if he could get far enough away, he could forget about Glory. Maybe New Mexico. Or Montana. Hell, that was no good. Even the North Pole wouldn't be far enough away for that.

He walked back to the barn, his mind thinking up— and immediately rejecting—ways to tell her he was leaving. It wasn't going to be easy. Dub had said she'd pitch a hissy fit when she heard the news.

If he knew Glory, that wouldn't be the half of it.

Glory kept looking for Ross all morning, but he didn't show up for the clinic. At nine o'clock she greeted and registered the first arrivals—two young sisters with their Connemara ponies. The girls were old hands at showing their ponies in jumping classes, and they also belonged to a local pony club that emphasized horse care. Therefore, the animals were in excellent condition and required only vaccinations and Coggins tests for equine infectious anemia. A negative test result for the highly contagious disease was a requirement for all horse shows.

Glory welcomed a steady stream of clients. All morning she filed horses' teeth, gave tetanus shots and ran tests. She suggested a diet for a fat old gelding and diagnosed a mild case of pulmonary emphysema in a sorrel mare. She advised the young owner and his father to avoid giving the horse dusty feeds, which only aggravated the problem, and to pasture her year-round so that she'd get plenty of fresh air.

As a final recommendation she warned them not to work the mare too hard. Since she belonged to a conscientious eleven-year-old who clearly doted on the animal, Glory was confident that her instructions would be followed to the letter.

During the next few hours, she was so busy she hardly had a chance to wonder why Ross hadn't shown up to help out as he'd promised. The hired hand he sent in his place had said only that "something had come up." After last night and Ross's remark about maybe never getting around to her, she couldn't help but worry.

Glory confirmed pregnancy in a little boy's pet burro and treated a Shetland pony for mange mites. She discussed nutrition, grooming, handling and schooling. Her patients included ponies and pintos, foals and fillies. Young horses, middle-aged horses and a few very old horses. Chestnuts and roans, buckskins and duns. She saw a lot of different kinds of horses, but they all had one thing in common—each was loved by a child.

She identified strongly with the young horse owners and won their confidence because she knew how to talk to them. Even though the parents were most often present also, she directed her advice and instructions to the children. She reminded them that they were the ones who were responsible for their pets, and her efforts were rewarded by small faces lit up with pride. The kids went away feeling they had made a new friend in Doc Roberts, and Glory found personal satisfaction in accomplishing what she'd set out to do.

By the end of the day she was exhausted but still worried about Ross. When she stopped by his house and found him gone, she became even more concerned. Back home, she cornered her parents in the kitchen and asked about him as she cleaned up at the sink. "Did Ross say where he was going?"

Dub and Ruby exchanged troubled looks. "No, honey, he didn't," Dub said. "Just that he had some business to attend to."

"How about some beef stew?" Ruby thought most problems could be solved by good stick-to-your-ribs food. She lifted the lid on the slow cooker, and a spicy aroma filled the room.

"No, thanks, Mama. I'm pretty tired. I think I'll go up to my room and rest."

As she departed, Glory overheard her mother say in a hushed voice, "Go up to her room and brood, is more like it. I just don't know what to do. I wish there was some way we could help."

"Ain't nothing us old folks can do, Mama," her father answered. "Young folks gotta work out their own problems, I reckon."

Ross showed up the next day, somewhat reluctantly it seemed to Glory, to drive everyone to Brody and Noelle's house, but he didn't say a word about where he'd spent Saturday. He asked how the horse clinic turned out, and she assured him it had been a success. He glanced uneasily at Dub, and both her parents stared out the windows. Ruby seemed pained not to be able to speak her mind about something, but she remained quiet and Ross tuned the radio to a country music station.

Glory wasn't sure what was going on, but she sensed a conspiracy. Before she could ask any questions, a whiskey-voiced female singer came on the radio belting out the words to a song called "Love and Other Long Shots," and Ruby said excitedly, "Isn't that the song Noelle's friend Darcy wrote?"

"I believe it is," Glory said. The song was beginning to receive quite a bit of airplay even though the singer was an unknown. Every time she heard it, she thought of Riley. It was too bad things hadn't worked out between him and the raven-haired Darcy.

Ross appeared to concentrate on his driving and avoided looking directly at Glory who was seated right beside him. As soon as the song ended, she leaned over and snapped off the radio.

He glanced over at her, and she was glad she'd finally figured out a way to get his attention. "You know, Ross, I don't mind you taking papers from the files, but I wish you'd return them when you're finished."

He was so disarmed by her smile that it was a few seconds before it dawned on him what she'd said. "I didn't take anything from the files, Doc."

She frowned thoughtfully. "That's strange. I was going to make some notations on High Flyer this morning, but his folder was empty."

"I distinctly remember you putting his charts back in that folder last week, after we discussed your concerns about him."

Glory shrugged. "That's what I thought, but it's empty now. I even checked the files of the two mares we bred him to. His papers weren't there."

"Maybe you accidently filed a folder in a folder. I'll help you look tomorrow."

"Lordy, do you think there really is a serious problem with Prescott's stallion?" Dub asked from the back seat. "That man calls me a couple of times a week to check on him."

"I don't know yet if it's a problem or not," Glory told her father. "But both mares, Jewel-of-the-Nile and Farmer's Folly, normally conceive after their first exposure. I was really surprised when neither of them showed signs of a pregnancy settling."

"Maybe High Flyer isn't quite the stud Prescott seems to think he is," Dub mused aloud. "How much do you know about the horse, Ross?"

"Not much. Only that he was a very successful racer in the American Quarter Horse Association and that he was retired from the circuit this year." He glanced in the rearview mirror at the older man. "Prescott's expecting to make another small fortune off standing him at stud. He's certainly in demand. We've had a lot of calls about the rates."

"He's pretty high-strung. That might have something to do with it," Glory pointed out. "*If* he has a problem, it may only be a temporary, psychological condition."

Her father sighed. "What about the ultrasound results on the mares?"

"Nothing showed up, no embryonic sacs. Ross and I decided to repeat the artificial inseminations, so I saved a sample and sent it off to be tested. Just to make sure."

Not one to sit quietly for long, Ruby put in her two cents' worth. "It isn't unusual for a mare not to breed the first time."

"No," Glory conceded. "But these two always have in the past. Since they've been coming to us for several years, I checked their records."

"Do you think High Flyer might be sterile?" Ruby asked.

"Lordy, I hope not," Dub remarked. "Prescott will be sure to blame it on us somehow. That man is driving me crazy with his phone calls, wanting to know if his baby has settled in, or if there's any problem he needs to know about."

"It's almost as if Prescott's expecting to hear the worst." Ross figured his naturally suspicious nature was working overtime, but he couldn't help thinking about all the "accidents" that had occurred since High Flyer came to the ranch. And now his papers were missing.

"I think he's more worried about my ability to handle the horse than anything else," Glory said with a laugh. "I have to tell you, I was worried about it at first. Flyer's so big and aggressive around the men, but he follows me around like a puppy dog."

Ross chuckled. "Bobby thinks he's finally figured out why High Flyer is such a gentleman when you come into the barn."

Glory loved the sound of his relaxed laughter and the twitching of his little dimple. Maybe she'd just

imagined the tension between him and her parents.
"How's that?"

"Bobby's theory is that it's because you almost always wear sneakers around the clinic. The rest of us wear boots and that puppy dog of a horse likes to nibble on your shoestrings."

Ruby giggled. "Sounds like he's just a big overgrown pet, but then animals always have taken to Glory. Remember the time she brought home that hairy rat from school?"

"Mickey was a gerbil not a rat," Glory reminded her.

"Looked like a rat to me. I think I was the only one on the farm who didn't cry at his funeral in the backyard a couple of months later. Poor little Glory wasn't much of a vet back in those days."

They all laughed and the subject was changed. The rest of the drive was spent on funny remembrances of Glory and her pet this or that. Once, when she reached across the seat to squeeze Ross's hand, he had squeezed it back before quickly returning it to the steering wheel. The warmth of his touch helped convince her that there was nothing wrong. She wouldn't even think about the sad look in his eyes.

That afternoon, after a delicious midday dinner, Ross sat in the Sawyer living room wondering why he'd agreed to come here and inflict this kind of pain on himself. He didn't belong at family gatherings, even if they all treated him as if he did. No matter how much he yearned for it, he could never be a part of this family, and now that he'd already started burning his bridges, he felt the sense of loss more than ever.

He didn't have time to brood, however, because five-year-old Dusty climbed onto his lap and handed him a crudely drawn picture of a stick horse and cowboy. "I drawed this for you, Ross."

Danny clambered onto the sofa beside him and gave him another, similar drawing. "Me, too."

"Thanks, boys. These are great pictures and I'll hang them on my wall as soon as I get home." He'd spent the past few hours trying not to stare at Glory. Now that he was leaving, it was as if he had to memorize her every move, and he was grateful for the diversion the twins provided.

Danny giggled behind his chubby fist. "You're 'sposed to hang 'em on the fridge, silly."

Ross smiled. "Okay, the fridge it is."

Dusty took up for his pal. "He didn't know that, Danny, on account of him not having any kids." He turned to Ross and grinned reassuringly. "You hang 'em on the fridge with magnets," he explained sagely, "until we draw you some new ones. Then you take the old ones and put 'em in a box and save 'em. See?"

"That's what Mommy and Gramaw Ruby do," Danny added.

Ross nodded. "That makes good sense."

"Good sense! From these two?" Glory scooped Danny up in her arms and sat down on the cushion next to Ross. She had spent the whole day watching him trying not to watch her and decided that he definitely seemed melancholy today. She wanted to grab his hand and drag him off some place where they could be alone. Where she could get to the bottom of his problem, where she could kiss him and hold him and love him.

But since that was out of the question at the moment, she had to be content to just be near him. She held the squirming little boy in her lap, tickling him, until he broke into a fit of giggles. "What these guys are full of is nonsense."

Dusty grinned. "Not me. Huh, Ross?"

"I'm afraid so." He grinned and tickled the now squirming child on his lap, too.

Finally the boys begged for mercy and promised to draw some pictures for Aunt Glory's fridge at the clinic. The moment they were released, they scampered off to their room to do just that.

Glory leaned back and smiled at Ross, who was busy studying the shiny tips of his boots. "Does Noelle look different to you?"

He figured it was safe to look at Noelle and glanced across the room where she, Dub, Ruby and Brody were deep in a conversation about some new racing stock. Noelle was perched on the arm of her husband's chair. They were never far apart, but that was nothing new, and he could see no change in her appearance. "Not really. Why?"

"It's just a feeling. I think they've got a secret."

"Everyone's entitled to those," Ross said uneasily.

"Not from me, they aren't," Glory said with a mock-sinister look. "We weren't all just invited out here for barbequed brisket and potato salad. They have something up their collective sleeve and I'm determined to find out what."

Ross glanced at the couple in question again. Brody and Noelle were holding hands, but they were always touching. He knew if Glory were his wife, he'd never get enough of touching her. "It's no secret how they feel about each other."

"I don't mean that. Look at the gleam in Brody's eyes and that dopey half grin he's had on his face all day," she pointed out. "Noelle, too, for that matter."

Ross considered it for a moment. "Maybe they're just wishing we'd all go home so they can be alone."

"Riley, we need your opinion about something." Glory hailed her other foster brother as he came inside from making an evening inspection of the barns. She patted the cushion beside her and was grateful for a chance to scoot even closer to Ross.

The whole family was proud of Riley and the new man he'd made of himself. There was only one thing Glory would change about him if she had her way. His loneliness. She knew he was still in love with the songwriter Darcy Durant. But the last time she'd asked, Noelle had told her that Darcy was still in Nashville.

"What's up?" Riley asked as he leaned back on the sofa.

"Don't you think Brody and Noelle are acting strangely?" she asked.

Riley didn't even glance in their direction. "Yeah," he agreed. "They've seemed a little out of it lately. But especially Brody."

Glory frowned. "What do you mean?"

"Take last night, for instance. I came home from Remington Park," Riley lowered his voice, "and we had five first-place winners out of six starters. I came over to give Brody my glowing report. He just sat there like a bump on a log, occasionally nodding and mumbling, 'That's good, Riley.' Then when I got up to leave, he walked outside with me and says, 'Oh, by the way, did we win any today?' Hell, I'd just spent fifteen minutes telling him that.''

"I hope it's nothing serious." Glory frowned, already worrying.

"Me, too. I asked him what was wrong, but he just grinned kind of goofylike and said things couldn't be more right." Riley glanced at Ross. "What do you think?"

Ross felt uncomfortable speculating about other people's secrets when he had so many of his own. "I think it's none of our business."

Just then Brody stood and pulled his wife up beside him, their arms and fingers entwined.

"Boys," Noelle called out to her sons, "would you please come in here for a moment?"

The children barreled into the room to stand by their parents. "Is it time to tell our secret, Daddy?" Dusty wanted to know.

Glory shot Ross an I-told-you-so glance and he smiled.

Danny looked thoughtful. "Secret?"

"You know." Dusty put his hands on his hips and shook his head. "About us having a baby."

"Oh, *that* secret."

The next thing Ross knew, Glory was hugging him and kissing his cheek in her excitement. He glanced around the room, embarrassed by his strong reaction to her touch. No one was paying any attention because everyone was talking at once and hugging and shaking hands and offering congratulations. By the time he realized it was safe to relax and enjoy Glory's exuberant affections, at least for the duration of the commotion, she had jumped up to bestow them elsewhere.

Watching the happy scene, Ross had to envy the love the family had for one another. If he could have handpicked his own family, this one would have been it. Every time they got together they generated a loving warmth and support that reached out to encompass everyone they came in contact with. Including him. How that would change if he stood up and revealed is own little secret.

Glory claimed to love him, and he dared to hope that the truth wouldn't matter to her or the others. No, he amended, she loved the man she thought he was. Every time he tried to sort out his feelings, his love for her became tangled up with his other emotions.

The only thing he knew for sure was that his life before her had seemed like pure hell and that a future without her loomed bleakly ahead of him.

As soon as the ruckus died down a little, Ross stood and offered his own heartfelt congratulations to the parents-to-be. It was a couple of hours before Dub finally started making noises about getting back to the ranch.

Ruby chattered all the way home about the new baby, and when Ross parked Dub's car in the driveway, she invited him in for coffee.

"I better not. I've got some paperwork to do," he hedged.

"It'll keep," she insisted. "I made a fresh batch of those fried pies this morning."

"Apricot?" he asked.

"Is there any other kind?"

Ross shrugged and followed them inside.

Still elated over Brody and Noelle's announcement, Glory wasn't ready for the night to end. On the drive home she'd tried to imagine what it would be like being married to Ross. Making babies with him. Sharing everything life had to offer. He'd seemed particularly distant today, but she knew he was concerned about the mares and High Flyer's possible infertility. There'd be plenty of time to talk to him—he wasn't going anyplace.

She set about brewing coffee while Ruby warmed the pies and got ice cream from the freezer. Dub and Ross sat down at the table, and Ruby set a platter of fried pies in front of them. "I'm so happy for Brody and Noelle."

"Me, too, and I can hardly wait for the baby to get here. I'm eager to get my hands on a newborn." Glory couldn't help fantasizing a bit about the child she and Ross would have. Someday.

"I wonder if they'll have a boy or a girl." Ruby poured coffee. "Wouldn't a little girl be nice? All ruffles and lace?"

"With ultrasound, you don't have to wonder," Glory told her as she dished up the ice cream.

"Noelle says they want to be surprised. I think that's sweet."

Dub and Ross shared a long-suffering look across the table, and Dub laughed. "If there's anything women like more than talkin' about babies, I sure don't know what it is."

Ross just sipped his coffee. His eyes met Glory's as she slid a bowl in front of him. Their gazes locked and her voice was husky when she said softly, just to him, "Unless it's having some of their own."

Her sensual wink made Ross choke, and he spluttered the hot brew back into his cup.

Thankfully a knock on the back door drew everyone's immediate attention, and he was saved from having to explain his embarrassment.

Glory opened the door and greeted one of their top hands. "Hi, Bobby, anything wrong at the barns?"

"Not really, I was looking for Ross."

"He's here, come in. Want some pie and coffee?"

Bobby stepped inside the door and removed his cowboy hat. "Thanks, but Mary's waiting supper on me."

Ross spoke up. "What's up, Bobby?"

"When I came home just now, Mary told me a man named Prescott came and loaded up his horse about an hour ago. She tried to get him to wait until she could call you folks, but he claimed he'd already squared his bill with Dub."

Bobby scratched his head. "Being Sunday and all, Mary was the only one on the place, what with me gone to town to check on my mother. She tried to call, but Brody said y'all had just left. So she sent me down here to check it out."

Ross and Dub exchanged worried glances. Not once during all of his phone calls had Prescott said anything about taking High Flyer home.

"I hope she did the right thing," Bobby said.

Glory spoke up reassuringly. "Mary did the only thing she could under the circumstances. Old man Prescott probably decided he didn't like the idea of a female vet after all." She followed him to the door and as he was leaving, she said, "Tell her not to worry."

"He didn't settle his bill. The nerve of that man pulling a sneaky thing like that," Ruby said indignantly. When Dub stood up, she asked, "Where are you going?"

"To phone Prescott."

"Dubhoney, he won't be back in Tulsa if he picked up his stallion only an hour or so ago," Ruby pointed out logically.

"I hope and pray he isn't," he called over his shoulder as he marched off the steps to the den.

An uneasy silence pervaded as they waited for Dub to return. When he did, he was noticeably pale.

"What took you so long?" Glory asked.

They all waited expectantly for Dub's answer.

"I had to call the sheriff. It looks like High Flyer has been stolen."

## Chapter Eight

The sheriff came out later that night. After talking to Dub and Ross, he interviewed Mary, but she wasn't certain about the make of the vehicle and hadn't thought to write down the license tag. All she knew for sure was that the horse trailer had been silver and the pickup truck had been a black late model. She didn't recognize the man claiming to be Prescott, and he'd been alone. However, she could describe him in detail.

Whoever had taken High Flyer, it wasn't Wade Prescott.

The sheriff took down the description and other information and said he and his deputies would try to get around to questioning the neighbors and employees of Phoenix Farm as soon as they could. He promised to devote as much time to the investigation as he could spare, but they didn't have much to go on. He couldn't, in good conscience, offer much hope of getting the animal back.

Prescott phoned the next day, threatening the ruination of Phoenix Farm's good name if his horse wasn't located and returned safely. He vowed to tell fellow horsemen how "irresponsible" Dub and Ross had been, and within two days several Tulsa clients, as well as a few local ones, had settled their debts and removed their animals from the premises.

On Tuesday news from the authorities was grim. The neighbors and employees had been questioned, but nothing new had turned up. No one had seen anything suspicious. There were thousands of pickups fitting Mary's description, and it would be impossible to check them all out. A dead end.

The sheriff surmised the crime had been committed by an organized horse-theft ring that his department had learned about from the state bureau of investigation. He figured High Flyer was long gone, probably taken to Mexico where illegally bred colts sired by winners fetched a handsome price if the proper contacts were made.

As upsetting as all this was to her, Glory spent what little free time she had trying to reassure her beleaguered parents. Further search of her files revealed that Flyer's papers, including his passport, were indeed missing, but she couldn't figure out how or when the thieves could have gotten into her office.

She longed to talk to Ross about her growing uneasiness over Flyer's disappearance. There was something strange about the case that she couldn't put her finger on yet, but it was just a feeling and she had nothing concrete to go on. Besides, Ross was so preoccupied with his own worries about the theft—

and something else that she'd hadn't figured out—that he was impossible to approach.

Dub and Ruby were highly distressed over the incident. Doubt and suspicion, when it came from clients they'd had for years, made them fear the loss of everything they'd worked for all their lives. Dub started smoking again and Ruby stopped chattering—ominous signs that made Glory concerned for their well-being.

When Brody and Noelle called to ask them to stay at their house Tuesday night with Dusty and Danny while they went to a horse show in Enid, she encouraged them to accept. She was in favor of anything that would get them out of the house and especially away from the constantly ringing telephone. It didn't take much to convince them they needed the respite, and she said goodbye to them before she left to answer a call about a sick horse on a neighboring farm.

Ross was on hand to see them off, and despite everything they'd been through for the past two days, he couldn't help grinning with affection as he tried to help Dub shoo Ruby into the car.

She wouldn't be hurried. "I left a casserole in the refrigerator and—"

"Why are you telling him all over again, Mama?" Dub turned to Ross. "I swear, this woman clucks around worse than a mother hen."

"That may be, Dubhoney, but it'll be bad news in the chicken house tonight if you don't humor me on this." She took a quick breath and began anew. "Now, as I was about to say, I left a note about your supper and Glory's. It's on the kitchen table, along with all the directions."

Dub opened the trunk and put a small case inside, then opened the passenger door. "Let's go, Mama, or we'll be late."

She glanced at her watch. "Oh, pooh, it's only four o'clock."

"I know, but you ain't in the car, either," Dub pointed out sarcastically.

"I will be," she insisted. Turning to Ross, she added quickly, "Glory should be home by five. She's gone over to the Snowbird Ranch. If she's not home by then you might want to call over there and check on her. The number's in that little doohickey by the phone. She shouldn't be late, it's only a colicky horse, and she said herself that it shouldn't take her too long."

"Knowing her, she'll probably stay and help walk that horse until it's completely recovered," Dub replied.

Ruby frowned. "Oh, I hope not. I worry about her driving alone on these rural roads after dark."

Dub patted her shoulder. "Glory's grown now, Mama."

"Even grown-ups can have car trouble," she insisted stubbornly.

"That's why she has that expensive cellular phone in her Blazer." When Dub had finally nudged his wife into the car, he asked Ross, "How come you haven't told Glory you're leaving?"

"What with all that's happened, I haven't had a chance. I plan to talk to her tonight." That was a task he was not looking forward to.

Ruby dashed away a tear and rolled down her window. "I declare, I don't know what we'll do without you, Ross. You always take such good care of us. We'll be home in time for supper tomorrow night, and there should be plenty of food left over for lunch tomorrow. Oh, I almost forgot—''

"Say goodbye, Ruby." Dub revved the engine, put the car into gear and sped down the driveway.

Ruby hung her head out the window and, cupping her hands around her mouth, called, "There's some apricot pies in the fridge."

Ross waved and then went to the barn to supervise the feeding and bedding down of the animals. He attended to some outside chores, all the while keeping an eye out for Glory's return.

The sheriff came by and talked to Mary again. This time her little boy Junior had some surprising information. Ross thought about the implications of that while he waited for Glory. When she hadn't returned by six o'clock, he chalked it up to some unforeseen problems she might have encountered with the Snowbird horse.

By seven he had a hard time concentrating on the new leads the sheriff's investigation had turned up, and by eight he'd given up completely and seated himself on the porch, ready to give her a piece of his mind when she did arrive. He fought the urge to call and check up on her, knowing she wouldn't appreciate being treated like a child out past curfew. But nine o'clock found him pacing the length of the porch and cursing Glory's lack of consideration.

By ten o'clock, Ross was frantic. Any number of horrible things could happen to a woman alone. Hell, according to the papers, they happened every day. He didn't care how mad his checking up would make her, he marched inside to call the Snowbird Ranch.

The ranch was only fifteen minutes away, and when he learned she'd left over an hour ago, his heart ham-

mered and he tasted bitter fear. Noticing the blinking
light on the answering machine, he recalled that Dub
always turned it on when he and Ruby were out of the
house. He gave a silent plea that he'd hear Glory's
voice. He wasn't disappointed.

"If anybody's there, it's me. My car's dead." Her
words floated out of the box, telling him where to find
her.

Ross practically ran out of the house, relieved that
she was all right. He made sure he had any tools he
might need, then jumped into his pickup and roared
off into the darkness.

Glory checked her watch for the hundredth time and
grimly noted that barely half an hour had passed since
she'd called the house. It was after ten and she'd been
sitting here twiddling her thumbs for over an hour. If
she'd started walking when the Blazer first conked out
on her, she could have been home by now.

Instead of sitting here in the dark, jumping out of
her skin every time a jackrabbit crossed the road. But
wasn't that the reason she hadn't ventured out? The
dark? It was deep and full of creaky night sounds,
with only a tiny sliver of pale moon in the wide night
sky. After years in a college town that never really
slept, she had enjoyed the quiet of the country. But
that was when she had company.

A whole hour and not one car had come down
either this godforsaken road or the one that crossed it
about a quarter of a mile away. Running late, she'd
decided to take a shortcut home, but the area was dark
and forbidding and, as far as she could tell, there were
no houses on this lonely stretch.

She had kept her lights on for a while, but had been forced to turn them off when they'd grown dim. She wanted to save the battery so she could signal a car by flashing her lights. So far, not one had passed.

The phone had been small comfort. What good was a cellular phone when no one was home? She'd left a message on her parents' machine even though she'd known they wouldn't be there. She'd called Ross and the number to the barns every five minutes, but no one had answered. Then she remembered everyone had gone to watch Bobby and Mary's oldest son play basketball. Ross was supposed to be holding down the fort, but where was he when she needed him?

She dialed again. Still no answer.

Glory hung up and stared down the road, praying for the welcome sight of headlights. A few minutes later she sighed with relief when she spotted some approaching. She switched her lights on and off to signal for help and didn't consider her vulnerability.

A beat-up old car pulled up beside the Blazer, and Glory rolled down her window. Smiling at the young man who got out, she said, "Wow, am I glad to see you!"

A flashlight beam pierced the darkness and Glory was momentarily blinded by its glare. A slightly slurred voice called, "Hey, Derek, looks like we got ourselves a lady in distress here."

Glory's smile faded when she realized her would-be rescuer had already finished more than the can of beer in his hand. She looked out the opposite window and saw a stocky-built blond teenager, his face blotched with acne, approach.

Good sense demanded she crank up the window and make sure all her doors were securely locked. She lifted the receiver of the phone and said loud enough for them to hear, "I've already called for help, so you can go wherever it was you were going."

"Hey, I thought you were glad to see us."

A ruddy face loomed at her window. "'Sides, we don't have any place to go." He stumbled and fell against the door.

The sudden thump startled Glory and she jumped in her seat. *Stay calm. Don't let them think you're frightened.* She wasn't really scared. She could handle this. They were just a couple of kids high on beer. So why was her heart pounding so painfully?

"Come on out of there, honey," Derek taunted. "We'll give you a beer."

"Thanks, but I don't really need your help. My brothers will be here any minute," she fabricated, hoping the thought of a number of approaching males might be enough to send them away.

No such luck.

Derek grinned menacingly. "Hey, Glen," he called to his companion, "bring the little lady a beer."

Glen fumbled with a six-pack and held up a can. "You'll have to roll down the window, doll face."

Glory shook her head vehemently. "Thanks anyway, but I'm not thirsty." She reached for the phone and frantically punched in Ross's number again. She was shaking so badly she misdialed and got the this-is-not-a-working-number lady.

"That's not very friendly," Derek taunted. "We're just trying to be of service."

The two boys laughed maniacally, but Glory failed to see the humor in the situation. She fought to remain calm by telling herself they were little more than children who were getting a big kick out of scaring her to death.

Soon anger began to replace fear. "Look, guys, you've had your fun, now run along. You don't look old enough to be driving, much less drinking, so get out of here before I call the sheriff."

Glen slapped his open palm on the hood of the Blazer and mouthed an ugly word at her.

Derek scowled. "Look, we're not stupid. If you could call the sheriff, you'd have already done it."

The boys began pounding on the Blazer, knocking on the window, rocking the vehicle between them. They yelled at her to come out and show them a good time or they'd have to come in and get her.

Glory considered calling 911. How fast could the dispatcher respond to a call from such an isolated spot? Only someone familiar with the area could find this road in such complete darkness. No one could get here in time. Just when she was beginning to think her fate was sealed, she saw headlights barreling down the road toward her.

Thank God. She was so glad to see another car that she didn't care if it contained Bigfoot himself. She banged on her horn, which emitted a sound vaguely reminiscent of a car with laryngitis. She switched her lights off and on.

She felt giddy with relief when Ross's pickup screeched to a halt directly in front of her vehicle, its bright lights illuminating the scene. Now it was Derek and Glen who squinted and turned away from the lights.

Emboldened by his sudden appearance, Glory rolled her window down a smidgen. "That's my brothers," she informed the gawking boys. "You'd better get out of here while you still can."

"It's only one man," Derek replied with a scowl. "There's two of us."

"Yeah," Glen agreed, but she noticed his voice was a bit shaky and that he'd edged closer to his car.

As Ross climbed out of the pickup, he pulled a tire iron from behind the seat. Something dark and dangerous had boiled up inside him when he saw those men rocking the Blazer and terrorizing Glory. Blood pounded thickly at his temples and anger overwhelmed his good sense. His throat tightened with the desire to protect her no matter what the cost.

Glory saw the look of pure rage on Ross's face as he approached, and was more afraid than she had been earlier. But now the fear was not for herself, it was for the foolish boys. And for Ross. She'd seen him mad before, but she'd never seen him like this. His normally gentle eyes glared with a hostility that touched her heart with ice.

Hefting the tire tool in his hand, Ross stood with his feet braced apart. "You children having fun?" he asked in a quietly menacing tone.

Derek began inching toward Glen's car. "Hey, man, we don't want no trouble." He raised his empty hands to attest to that fact.

"That's not what it looked like to me." Ross stared down the frightened boys.

"We were just kidding around, man," Glen whined.

"I've seen your kind before," Ross told them. "You enjoy harassing defenseless women. Does it make you feel like big men?"

There was something in Ross's tone, in his stance, his manner, that was unrecognizable to Glory. Something violent that she'd never sensed in him before. Whatever it was, she knew that once it was unleashed, nothing could help those boys. "Get out of here," she yelled at them. "Run."

After a scrambling retreat, they gained the relative safety of their car and the engine started with a roar. Whatever it was that had held Ross in check snapped, and he raced to the car. Raising the tire iron in both hands, he brought it down on the trunk with a sickening crunch of metal. The car's driver accelerated, and the old bomb zoomed down the road, flinging a shower of dust and gravel on Ross.

He threw the bar to the ground and kicked it away from him. Frustration and anger rumbled up inside him like a volcano about to erupt, and he fought to contain it. These dark feelings were terrifying in their intensity. He'd experienced them before, but he'd managed to keep them under control for years. Now he cursed himself for revealing them to Glory. His breathing was deep and shallow, and his body trembled from the effects of ebbing adrenaline.

Glory fumbled with the door lock and stumbled out of the Blazer. She approached Ross warily and tentatively laid her hand on his arm. "Ross?" she asked softly. "Are you all right?"

He pulled her into his arms and hugged her to him, careful not to squeeze her as tightly as he wanted to, afraid he might hurt her. "Oh, God. If I hadn't gotten here when I did, those two might have..." He choked off the rest of the words, the thought too painful to bear.

Glory wrapped her arms around his neck, clinging to him. "But you did get here. It's all over now," she soothed him, careful to keep the tears out of her voice. "I'm fine."

Ross wanted to stand this way forever, with Glory safe in the shelter of his arms. He wanted to spend his life protecting her, but now, more than ever, he knew that what she most needed protection from was him. He took her arms from his neck and turned her toward his pickup. "Get in, you're going home."

"What about the Blazer?"

"I'm taking you home, we'll worry about it tomorrow."

During the ride, she tried to explain what had happened, but Ross didn't respond. He just gripped the steering wheel and stared down the dusty road. "I don't think those boys would have really hurt me," she finished lamely.

Ross couldn't take it anymore. He snapped, "You don't have any idea what human beings are capable of."

"And you do, I suppose?"

"Yes, dammit, I do." After that vehement comment he lapsed into silence again.

Glory grew more upset with each minute that he refused to talk to her, and by the time they reached the house, she'd worked herself into an anger that nearly matched his own. She stomped up to the front door and fumbled in her pocket for her key. Ross reached around her and pushed it open.

"Wait here until I have a look around," he instructed curtly. "I left in such a hurry, I forgot to lock up."

"This is silly," she yelled after him. "Are you going to look for monsters in the closets because of what happened tonight?"

He ignored her and disappeared into the house, flipping on lights as he went. When he came back and gave the all clear, she marched up the stairs. She paused on the landing and called down to him. "I've had a long day and I need a shower. But don't leave, we've got some talking to do."

"You can say that again," he grumbled.

Glory hurried through her shower, and while she was looking for something to put on, it occurred to her that they were finally all alone in the house. True, recent events weren't exactly conducive to romance, but whatever Ross's problem was, hopefully he'd had time to simmer down.

Or maybe it would be to her advantage if he hadn't. She'd tried for years to get him worked up to the kind of fiery passion she'd glimpsed in him tonight. All she had to do was rechannel it in her direction. And to do that, she needed the right outfit.

She rummaged around in her cedar chest until she found just the thing. In an optimistic moment, she'd bought the white satin ballet gown and matching kimono for her trousseau. Since Ross was the man she hoped to marry someday, what harm could come from him seeing it a little early?

She sprayed perfume on the inside of each elbow and at the base of her throat. As an afterthought, she squirted some behind her knees. She fluffed out her hair and took a long, critical look at herself in the mirror.

Not bad. The gown was a shiny confection iced with lace, and spaghetti straps brought the demure bodice well above her breasts. That was good, she didn't want to be too obvious. A lacy inset bordered her hips atop a double-tiered skirt of chiffon that flowed nearly to

her ankles. The white satin kimono had dropped
shoulders, elbow-length sleeves and a matching tie belt
that she adjusted loosely for effect.

When she heard Ross in the kitchen, she went directly into the living room and arranged herself on the
sofa. When she was satisfied that she looked subtly
provocative, she called out to him to join her. She was
tired of being ignored, or worse, treated like a baby
sister by the man she loved. Tonight he would have to
take her seriously as a woman.

Ross exploded into the room, barely managing not
to spill the two mugs of coffee he carried. "Do you
have any idea how worried I was tonight. When I saw
those thugs..." His words trailed away as he stepped
into the room. He took in her artfully displayed
beauty and the smoky look in her eyes and swallowed
hard.

What kind of game was she playing now? If she
thought a sexy nightgown could affect him...Ross
gave himself a mental shake. Damned if it didn't seem
to be working. It took everything in him to keep from
rushing to her side and taking her into his arms and
doing all the things he wanted to do but knew he
shouldn't.

Glory smiled. "Let's try to forget all that. Nothing
happened. I'm fine. You're fine. We're together.
Alone."

"That's not the point."

She patted the sofa beside her and beckoned him to
join her. "Oh, I think that's exactly the point."

"Don't you know what could have happened? You
could have been raped. Or killed."

"Oh, Ross." Glory gasped softly, suddenly realizing the extent of the danger she'd been in. "Please stop. You're frightening me all over again."

"I'm sorry," he said, and his anger dissolved into guilt at her distress. "Don't be afraid of me. I'd never hurt you."

Driven to desperate measures of deceit, Glory decided to take advantage of the situation. She dropped her face into her hands. "I'm sorry," she cried.

Ross couldn't bear to be the cause of her tears. He crossed the room, put down the coffee cups and sat beside her.

"Are you still mad at me?" she asked, swiping at her crocodile tears.

Taking her hand in his, he caressed it and whispered raggedly, "I could never be mad at you."

Glory flung her arms around his neck. He moaned deeply as he pulled her into his arms. A moan as primitive and unrestrained as her whimper escaped when their lips found each other. His probing tongue filled her with rivers of desire, and she gave herself up to the sensation. Tenderly she stroked the length of his jaw and reveled in the feel of his skin.

Here in Glory's arms, with his lips on hers, Ross could forget about the sordidness of the past. When he held her, everything was new and sweet and wondrous. All he could think about was her and the way she made him feel.

"Oh, God, I want you," he murmured against her mouth. Then he captured her hair in one hand and kissed her throat. His hands slid inside her kimono to caress her back as he brushed his lips over her eyes and cheeks before trailing back to her mouth again.

Glory sighed as his fingers slid over her bare shoulder, anticipating other, more intimate caresses. The whisper-soft touch held a magic all its own, and she trembled when he eased her back among the cushions. They were so close now she could feel the heat of his body, and she welcomed the intense desire she aroused in him.

Ross was drowning, long past logic and reason. He gave his heart full rein to lead him where it would. When her lips parted under his, he knew it wasn't a submission, but an equal response to her own fervent need. His hands found her breasts and cupped them lovingly, teasingly. He moaned when her hands skimmed down his throat and tugged apart the pearl snaps on his shirt. The popping sound was loud in the quiet room.

"You can't know how long I've wanted to do that," she whispered as she pulled the shirt out of his jeans. "How long I've waited to feel your skin against mine." Her hands fanned out over his chest, playing in the soft hair there, sliding slowly down until she encountered his belt buckle.

"Make love to me, Ross," she urged, her voice as sexy and deep as her kisses and just as passionate. "I want my first time to be with you. Tonight. Now."

Ross groaned in an agony of uncertainty. First time? He should have known, and truth to tell, he had. It took every ounce of willpower he possessed to pull her hands away from his belt, but somehow he managed.

Even as he jumped to his feet, Ross was resnapping his shirt, his fingers shaking so badly he barely managed. He could still feel the warmth of her hands on him, the softness of her lips.

Glory watched, somewhat dazed, as he paced the length of the room and raked his fingers through his hair. He paused and turned back to gaze at her.

She looked like a goddess—her kiss-swollen lips, her flushed face, her heavy-lidded eyes. Her breasts peeked sassily at him through that froth of lace, and her long slender legs showed clearly through the fine material.

She wanted him and there was nothing, no one, to stop him from having her. They had the whole house to themselves, the whole night. As his head cleared, Ross remembered why he had to stop. His voice was gruff when he spoke. "Fix your clothes."

"What's wrong?" She made no move to straighten the revealing garment.

"You're a virgin."

"Everyone has to start sometime."

"Not with me, they don't."

"Why not?"

"I assume you've been saving yourself for your husband."

"I've been saving myself for you, Ross."

"Don't say that," he groaned.

"It's true."

"You don't know anything about me."

"Then tell me, dammit!"

"You have no idea how grisly the skeletons in my closet are. I've done things that I can't forget. Things that would make a difference in how you feel about me."

"I don't care what you've done." Glory looked up at him. "How bad can they be? You could never do anything that would make me think less of you."

"I only wish that were true," he replied sadly.

"You were so young when you came here, your past can't possibly be too decadent. You like to act tough, but you've got a soft, generous heart and you're a good man. The best."

She made a feeble attempt at levity. "Oh, for heaven's sake. It's not as though you killed somebody."

Ross's facial muscles tensed and his eyes darkened. "That shows how little you do know."

The look on his face frightened her. She pulled him down onto the sofa beside her. "Ross? Don't you think it's time you told me everything?"

# Chapter Nine

Once Ross started talking, he couldn't stop. He'd already decided to tell Glory about his plans to leave and he did. He told her that and much, much more.

"I grew up in a small town where everyone's business was public knowledge, so right away my unwed mother and I were different from the so-called decent folks," he said sarcastically. "It soon became clear that I didn't fit in. I liked school, but the other kids wouldn't leave me alone so I ducked out. I hung around with like companions and got a reputation as a troublemaker."

Ross didn't mince words. It was important to him that Glory know exactly where he was coming from. When he glanced at her, he saw only tenderness in her eyes.

"Go on," she urged him.

"By the time I was sixteen, I was a walking textbook case of petty juvenile delinquency. I went one step too far and ended up serving nine months in a detention center.''

Glory felt empathy for the boy Ross had been. ''What happened?''

''A guy approached me and asked if I'd like to make a hundred bucks by driving a truckload of steers to Louisiana. I jumped at the chance to make some honest money, but I was picked up at the state line for transporting stolen property. When I finished serving my time, I came home and found my mother was seeing a rich rancher's son. Only problem was, he liked to beat up on women.'' Ross's words turned bitter. ''Maybe that's what they saw in each other—he needed a victim and she was ever willing to be one.''

Glory wasn't sure what to say, but she knew it was important to keep Ross talking. Talking until he'd purged the past completely. Maybe then they could get on with their lives. ''Did you try to talk to her about it?''

''It didn't do any good. She thought he was her salvation, but I hated him and didn't mind telling him so. One night I came home and he had her on the floor, hitting and kicking her. Yelling and calling her names. I couldn't stand it, and something just snapped inside me. You have to believe me,'' he said fiercely, ''even though I'd been in trouble before, even served time, I never thought of myself as a bad person. I'd never been violent or hurt anyone.''

''Of course you're not a bad person.'' Glory hurried to reassure him when she saw the haunted look in his eyes.

''That night I just lost it. I grabbed the bastard by the shirt and even though he was a lot bigger than me, I threw him against the wall.''

She held her breath, waiting for Ross to continue.

When he did, it was in a deathly quiet voice. "He died that night of a coronary embolism resulting from the head injury, and I was charged with first-degree manslaughter." He looked up, expecting his confession to elicit shock and revulsion.

Glory was indeed shocked, not for the reasons Ross might have supposed, but by the injustice. "But it was an accident," she cried.

"That's not how the authorities saw it."

"What about your mother?"

"She died a few weeks later. You know, I asked her once why she put up with that man, why she took his insults and black eyes. Know what she said? Because she loved him." Ross's laugh was hard. "She died because she was afraid of not being loved."

She touched his face gently. "Oh, Ross, if only you had told me before."

He went on, eager to get this over with. "It hurt that my love didn't count, so I guess my feelings got buried along with her. That was a good thing, considering I spent the next three years in prison."

"You were in prison?" she asked quietly, horrified to think of him in such an awful place.

The unshed tears in Glory's eyes told Ross more than her words ever could have. Now she would hate him. "The trial was a joke. Because I had a juvenile record, things stacked up against me pretty fast. A go-getter public defender became interested in my case and got the charges reduced to involuntary manslaughter. Given the extenuating circumstances, I probably wouldn't have served more than a year in a correctional facility, but the dead man's father used his influence and I was sentenced to ten years in the state prison.''

"You were just a child." The wrongness of what had happened to him, the waste of young life, hurt Glory deeply. When other boys his age were graduating high school, Ross had been facing incarceration. She waited for him to go on, and when he didn't, she put her arms around him. "You don't have to tell me about it if you don't want to."

He pulled out of her embrace. "I have to—it's past due. The experience had a sobering effect on me. I'd been pretty stupid, but I was smart enough to realize that I'd just thrown away ten years of my life. I vowed to serve my time and never again see the inside of a cell. I was a prisoner, but I refused to be a criminal. Sometimes it was hard to remember that when I had to fight to keep myself whole.

"Lucky for me, the prison psychologist was sympathetic to my case, and he helped me make the most of my time by getting the education I'd squandered. I studied and passed a high school equivalency test and qualified for college correspondence courses. Ironically, while I was behind bars, education opened up the world to me for the first time."

"It took a lot of strength to do what you did," she said with conviction.

"No. I was driven by fear. Fear that I'd spend my whole life in prison like so many of the men around me. I started reading and studying about quarter horses, and even though my only experience had been at a carnival pony ride when I was five, I knew that when I got out I wanted to work with horses."

"You were there for three years?" she asked.

"It seemed like a hundred. My attorney knew I'd been railroaded, and he got one of the original jurors to testify in a jury-tampering hearing. He managed to get me a new trial and I got out with time served."

"What did you do then?" Glory was still having trouble reconciling the Ross he said he was with the Ross she knew him to be. He'd survived an experience that would have scarred lesser men for life, and he'd come out on top.

"I left prison determined to put the past behind me. But when I tried to get work on area ranches, I found out real quick that you never quit paying for your mistakes. No one wanted to hire an ex-con, so I drifted from town to town looking for a place. I finally hitchhiked up the interstate and that's how I ended up here."

Glory remembered Ross as he'd been when he first arrived at Phoenix Farm. Sullen and embittered, he'd adopted a lone-wolf attitude to protect himself from the pain of rejection. The stony facade she'd mistaken for a lack of feelings had been his way of keeping distance between himself and anyone who might care about him.

He feared his anger, his love, all his emotions, because he worried that he couldn't control them. Oh, Ross. Her heart went out to him, to the boy whose only crime had been trying to protect his mother. Now that she understood him, now that she knew the secrets he'd kept hidden so many years, she loved him more than ever.

"I told Dub everything because I was tired of having the past catch up with me," Ross was saying. "He was the first man to give me what I wanted. A chance. He gave me my life back and I'll never forget that."

At first Glory was stunned that her father had also kept secrets from her. But upon reflection, she understood his silence. At thirteen she had no business knowing about Ross's life. A child could never have appreciated what he'd been through. Later, it had been up to Ross to tell her and he'd been unable to.

"Is this why you've refused my love, Ross?" she asked.

He gripped her shoulders and held her firmly. "I can't love you, don't you see? I wouldn't be fair to you. You don't know what I'm capable of, what I might do if provoked. Tonight when I saw those boys harassing you, I wanted to hurt them." Horror and revulsion underscored his words.

"Ross, what you did tonight was no criminal response," she cried. "You were trying to protect me from what appeared to be a clear and present danger. You can't hold your feelings in for years and not expect them to explode sooner or later. And you can't go on blaming yourself for something that happened so long ago. It isn't healthy. Let it go. It can only stand between you and happiness."

"Happiness?" Ross asked derisively.

"Don't you think you deserve to be happy at last?" she asked softly.

"I don't think you deserve a man like me."

His stubbornness scared her. She wouldn't let him ruin what they could have. "Dammit! Will you stop with all the crying violins? Stop pitying yourself. Okay. You made a mistake, but that was a long time ago and you were very young. You were wrong, but you paid for it. Give it up!"

"I can't, Glory." Ross's eyes were filled with an anguish she'd never before seen in any human being.

"I can't." He got up and headed for the door, but she wouldn't let him go.

"It doesn't matter to me," she told him.

The weight in Ross's soul lifted a little, hope bloomed a little. But he had to ignore it. "I'm not the man you fell in love with."

"That's the dumbest thing I ever heard. You are you, Ross. Because of what you did or in spite of it. I don't care. I love you. Nothing that came before us or between us means as much to me as you do."

Her words were so strongly felt, so vehement that he could only stare at her in wonder. Did she mean it? "You can say that now, but what about years from now? How will you feel when you have to explain to your children that instead of going to college, daddy went to prison? How will it look to your clients if they know your husband is an ex-con? Loving me could affect your career, or hadn't you thought of that?"

"I don't care what other people think."

"Well, dammit, Glory, you should." Ross felt his heart rip apart. "That's why I have to leave. So you can forget me."

She turned her tear-streaked face up to him. After thirteen long years, he'd finally called her by name, eschewing the impersonal nicknames he favored for the distance they provided. And he'd cursed her in the same breath. This wasn't the way things were supposed to end.

No. It wouldn't end here. "This isn't about the past. This is about trust. Why do you have so little faith in me?"

"What are you talking about?" Ross was confused. He was doing the right thing, wasn't he?

"You don't know me, or you'd realize that I could never hold the past against you. Ross, don't you love me enough to trust me?"

He wished he knew some way to show her that it had nothing to do with the depth of his love. "Glory, I won't stay here and let you throw your life away on me."

"I'm not throwing away anything. Haven't you been listening? I love you."

He looked at her blankly, trying to believe her words.

"You still don't get it, do you? You belong with me and I belong with you. If ever in the whole history of lovers, two people were perfect for each other, it's you and me. We've known each other so long. So well. No one else could give us what we can give each other. What do I have to do to convince you of that?"

Ross stood rooted to the spot, unable to move for fear he'd break the magic spell of her words. This was what he'd dreamed about. Casting away the past. Loving Glory. Being loved by her. The dream had been a part of his life for so long. Now that it seemed to be coming true, he didn't know what to say.

"Well!" she demanded.

He opened his arms to her, and with that simple gesture, Ross shrugged off the shameful weight of the past. The years of deceit, the dark secrets. Looking over his shoulder and worrying that someone would be there pointing an accusing finger at him.

As he basked in the warmth of Glory's loving declarations, he felt his past slip away, felt it lose the power to hurt him and steal his happiness. Relief poured through him like a cleansing spring rain, and he felt reborn.

Glory was right. He had paid for the past long enough. He deserved the future. *They* deserved it. "Kiss me," he said softly. "That might convince me."

Glory rushed into his arms, only too happy to fulfill his heartfelt request. She covered his face with kisses and couldn't stop until they were both laughing and hugging and crying a little, too.

After a few minutes, he cupped her face in his hands. "There's something else I have to tell you."

His voice was so grim that it frightened her all over again. "What is it?"

"The sheriff came by while you were out at the Snowbird Ranch. He talked to Mary again, and this time her little boy Junior was there. He'd been in bed when she was questioned the first time. He claims he saw a second man hunkered down in the horse trailer the day High Flyer was stolen."

"But the boy's only seven years old. Is he sure?"

"He's sure. All along I've suspected Harvey Tate had something to do with this, but I didn't know what. Junior claims it was Harvey in the trailer. I suspect Prescott knows something he's not telling."

"Prescott?"

"Think about it. If he weren't involved, why would he be causing so much trouble for Dub? The man's got something to hide, and I've got to find out what it is."

"No." Glory clutched his arm. "Let the authorities handle it."

"Harvey's probably out of their jurisdiction by now. If the law doesn't recover High Flyer, Phoenix Farm will suffer. Dub and Ruby will suffer. I owe it to them to do everything I can to straighten this mess out."

"But I don't want you to go away. Not now. I'm afraid."

"What are you afraid of?" he asked as he stroked her cheek.

"That I've dreamed all this. That you might change your mind about me. That you won't come back." The words poured out of her in a rush.

"I'll be back, Glory. You can count on that. In the meantime, I want you to think about what I've told you tonight. I want you to be sure it doesn't matter—"

"I've already told you—"

"I know. But give it some time to sink in. Think about it. Be absolutely certain." He touched her lips with his fingertips to prevent her from speaking. "Don't say anything more now. Wait."

She put her arms around his neck and hugged him tightly. "I'll wait forever, Ross. For you."

Their gazes locked, and she looked so sincere that his throat tightened with emotion. When he read the look of love shining so brightly in her eyes, he felt a primitive urge to sweep her into his arms and carry her away to a place where they would be alone for the rest of their lives.

Instead he lowered his head and traced her lips with his tongue. Her mouth was hot and sweet and as hungry as his own. Their wildly hammering hearts beat in unison.

Ross was so high on the moment that he kissed her again and again. Somewhere inside him a dam broke, and long-suppressed yearning drowned his formidable self-control.

Finally he buried his face in her hair, and Glory savored the feel of his fast, warm breath on her neck.

Ross had always kept his emotions in check, and now she reveled in this new urgency in his response. She tenderly cupped his cheeks with her hands, and his skin was warm and exciting beneath his fingertips. "I love you, Ross Forbes. I'll never stop loving you."

His fingers covered hers. "I love you, too." He stood up, knowing he had to leave before he acted on the powerful feelings she'd awakened in him. "I'd better go."

Glory understood and admired what Ross wanted to do. He had just this one more debt to repay, then he could come to her freely. "You just be darn sure you come back," she commanded, still a bit afraid to let him go.

"I'll be back," he promised.

The next day, Glory had to concentrate to keep her mind on her work. She had no problem while she was tending to the horses, but as soon as she returned to her office and settled down with a stack of paperwork, her thoughts started to wander.

She replayed those last minutes with Ross, alternately analyzing and savoring them over and over again. All the time she was making entries on medical charts, she was thinking about the future and the happily ever after she would have with him.

Dub and Ruby returned late in the afternoon, and she explained everything that had happened while they were gone, sparing no details save those too intimate to share. They didn't hear from either Ross or the sheriff that day, but the next morning, the Robertses had a surprise visitor.

Oren Davis was an investigator for the company that insured High Flyer. Prescott was demanding settlement, but the company wasn't satisfied and it was Davis's job to follow up on all leads. He was a stocky middle-aged man with a steel-gray crewcut and he was loaded for bear. He was also looking for Ross.

Dub offered the man a cup of coffee but little useful information. "Ross took some vacation time," was his answer to Davis's inquiries.

Glory and Ruby exchanged troubled glances. Glory knew her father would not say or do anything to jeopardize Ross's own private investigation. Not until they found out what this man wanted with him.

Davis frowned. "Where did he go?"

"I don't rightly know," Dub said evasively. "He didn't give me his itinerary."

Davis scribbled in his notebook. "When do you expect him back?"

Dub shrugged. "I reckon he'll come back when he comes."

Davis's sigh showed his exasperation. "Mr. Roberts, I think it would be in your best interests to answer my questions truthfully. I'd hate to put it in my report that you—"

"What my father means," Glory interrupted, "is that Ross had two weeks' vacation coming. Since he didn't tell us where he was going, we can't in all honesty expect him back before those two weeks are up."

The man nodded. "And when will that be?"

"Well, let's see," Ruby put in helpfully. "He left yesterday, on a Wednesday. So he should be back a week from next Wednesday. He's very conscientious." She drew a breath and went on. "Isn't he, Dubhoney? We were just talking the other day about how lucky we are to have a man like him working for us. He's never missed a day of work, except for that one day when he had a real bad case of the sniffles when he fell in the pond and—''

''Mrs. Roberts,'' Davis quickly intervened. ''I've been investigating this case, and I've checked with the officials. Are you all aware that Ross Forbes has a record?''

''We are,'' Dub said calmly. ''Ross has done nothing wrong here. He's never given me a minute's worry, nor any reason to doubt his integrity. We trust him completely.''

''I hope you feel that way after I tell you the things I found out about him.'' Davis frowned thoughtfully, then proceeded to read aloud from the paper he fished from his briefcase. When read coldly like this, Ross's list of misdemeanors and more serious crimes sounded damning.

Glory wanted to tell Davis why Ross had done those things. Davis didn't know that Ross's mother had been little more than a child herself. That she'd gone from man to man while Ross struggled to grow up on his own. Any way he could.

''He was just a kid,'' Dub put in loyally. ''He had no father to guide him.''

''A lot of people grow up without fathers, Mr. Roberts,'' Davis insisted. ''They don't all resort to crime.''

''I'd hardly call joyriding and smoking behind a Dumpster a life of crime,'' Dub argued.

*Way to go, Daddy,* Glory silently commended.

''Maybe not,'' Davis admitted grudgingly. ''But that's certainly what I'd call murder.''

''Ross didn't murder anyone,'' Glory cried. ''It was an accident. The man was beating his mother so badly she died.''

Davis looked up, surprised. "So you know about that?"

"Of course, we know about it," she said. "The charge against Ross was reduced to involuntary manslaughter. He served his time and paid his debt to society, so I don't want to hear your accusations."

"The circumstances surrounding the crime are irrelevant," Davis continued. "And his record does make him a prime suspect in this case." He shifted his papers. "Forbes made a very large deposit to his bank account a few days ago. That and his convenient disappearance is enough to raise serious questions."

"Ross has done nothing wrong," Glory repeated stubbornly.

"Maybe not." He looked directly at Dub and swept his papers into his briefcase. "But I hope I can expect full cooperation from you and your employees. Otherwise I hate to think of the repercussions this could have on you and your family. Not to mention your business concerns."

"Of course." Dub was suddenly solemn.

"What a hateful man," Ruby observed as soon as the door closed behind the investigator. "How dare he come in here and start accusing people."

Glory lifted her chin. "I don't care what he says. Nothing can make me doubt Ross. He's not involved in the theft."

"Of course he's not, honey." Dub patted her hand.

"Things are going all crazy." Ruby sobbed into her apron. "What are we going to do?"

Glory had definite ideas about that. Ross loved her and he was coming back. She had to remember that. "We're going to plan a wedding."

# Chapter Ten

They didn't hear from Oren Davis again and they assumed he returned to Tulsa. The sheriff phoned a couple of times, but he didn't have much to report. They tried to carry on business as usual, but Glory knew her parents were worried about the continued fallout from the theft. They'd lost a few more of their newer customers, but the old regulars—the ones who knew Dub and Ross too well to question their honesty—hung in there, offering support and encouragement.

Glory had received the news back from the lab confirming her suspicions about High Flyer's infertility. She wished Ross would call so that she could share the news with him. It might help if he knew that Prescott did indeed have ample motive for wanting his horse out of the way. She felt strongly that the problem was a temporary one and hoped nothing bad had happened to the stallion.

But Ross didn't call and Glory's spirits were low. The horses seemed to sense the gloomy atmosphere and were restless and uncooperative. That made even her lightest chores a task. She couldn't help but wonder where he was and what he was doing. Not even during the years she'd been away from Phoenix Farm had she missed him so intensely.

Late Saturday afternoon the whole farm was alerted when Ross's pickup truck pulled into the driveway. He backed the horse trailer he was towing up to the stables, and several hands ran out of the barn to unload its passenger.

High Flyer.

Glory heard the commotion and dashed out of her office, sprinting across the grounds to where Ross was speaking in low tones to Dub. Her father was shaking his head in disbelief as she picked up the thread of their conversation.

"You mean to tell me, Prescott was in on the whole thing?" Dub asked incredulously.

"Yeah." Ross took off his hat and swiped his arm across his face. He looked up then and saw Glory running toward him. Her shining eyes, her radiant smile, her haste, all told him that she'd missed him. That she still wanted him. His heart leaped.

When she stepped into his arms, he dipped his head for a quick welcoming kiss. "I missed you," he told her.

"Talk fast, we have some unfinished business," she said with a grin.

Ross acknowledged her with a dimpled smile before turning back to Dub. "He'd talked to Harvey when he was here before and paid him to arrange some kind of 'accident' in which Flyer would either be killed or injured so badly that he'd have to be put down."

"That way he could collect on the insurance, which he figured was a lot more valuable than an infertile stallion," Dub surmised.

Ross nodded grimly and squeezed Glory's hand.

She wanted to get Ross alone so she could tell him how much she'd missed him the past few days. Now that the horse was safe, the story of his rescue could wait. There were more important matters to be discussed.

But Dub seemed unaware of her impatience and went right on talking. "That explains why Harvey was so negligent."

"It wasn't negligence," Ross said. "It was all calculated. Harvey just happened to be a prime candidate for Prescott's deal. I've got to say one thing for Prescott. He sure understands character. If he'd said a word to any of the other hands, we would have known about the scam immediately."

Glory noticed how haggard Ross looked. He hadn't shaved for several days, and his clothes were rumpled and well-worn. He'd evidently been through a lot, and all she wanted to do was comfort him. She ached with the need to touch him, kiss him.

"Flyer appears to be in good shape physically," she observed. "If his problem really is psychological, as I suspect, he may recover in time."

Dub took off his hat and slapped his thigh. "Dang! To think that fool Prescott was willing to destroy a beautiful animal like this without checking further. Nothing gets my goat like that kind of stupidity."

"He was more interested in money than in his horse," Ross said. "That's why he was willing to sell him to me. Cheap."

"You bought High Flyer?" Glory asked incredulously.

"I couldn't let Prescott get his hands on him again. Besides," he added with a grin, "he needed the cash for bail money."

Dub approached Ross and clapped him on the back. "Thanks for everything, son. Recovering Flyer and proving Prescott was responsible will go a long way toward clearing our good name and putting Phoenix Farm back on the map."

"Don't mention it," Ross said wearily.

"You look done in, boy."

"I haven't slept much since I left," he admitted.

Dub finally noticed the looks of longing on Glory's and Ross's faces. "One more question, then I'll let you two talk. How'd you find Harvey?"

"The time I spent in prison taught me a lot about how the criminal mind works, and I used that knowledge to figure out what was going on. I suspected Prescott might be in on it, since Harvey wasn't smart enough to pull off something like this on his own. So I staked Prescott's place and waited for Harvey to get greedy."

"And he did?" Dub wanted to know.

"Oh, yeah. He'd already taken Prescott's money to do away with the horse, but that wasn't enough. He and an accomplice stole Flyer and his papers and planned to sell him illegally in Mexico. But they needed cash for the contacts and before they left, Harvey turned up at Prescott's place again, demanding some of the insurance settlement to keep his mouth shut. That's when I stepped in."

He went on to tell them how he'd already contacted the authorities in Tulsa and spoken to Oren Davis. Wade Prescott and Harvey Tate had been arrested that morning for attempting to defraud the insurance company and were in the Tulsa county jail awaiting arraignment. "We'll probably be asked to testify in the case against them," he said.

"That'll be a pleasure," Dub said with a grin.

"Best of all, because of the information I got from Tate, the authorities think they might have a lead that can help them crack that horse-theft ring."

"That's great, Ross," Glory said.

"Yeah, it is. Davis told me there was some question about how my bank account was suddenly so inflated," Ross went on. "I think I should explain that."

Glory looked stricken. "You don't have to explain a thing. We never doubted you. We never believed a word Mr. Davis said."

"She's right, Ross," Dub confirmed.

"I want to get everything out in the open." He looked down at Glory, and the love he felt for her shone in his eyes. "I don't want any more shadows between us."

She didn't speak. She didn't have to.

Ross began. "For the past fourteen years, I've spent very little of the money I earned. I never needed or wanted anything that I couldn't find right here. So I saved it and bought certificates of deposit when I accumulated enough to do so.

"I was so worried about the past that I didn't dare to dream of the future. But somewhere along the line I started thinking I might be able to buy you out, Dub, if the day ever came when you and Ruby wanted to retire. After all you've done for me, it seemed kind of presumptuous to talk about those hopes, so I kept them to myself. I was satisfied just to be here, to be your right-hand man.''

"You've been a hell of a lot more than that, Ross," Dub said fiercely.

Ross acknowledged Dub with a grin and turned to Glory. "Then you came home and shook things up. All of a sudden I couldn't think of anything but the future. When I saw you again, it was a shock to realize that I loved you—that I'd always loved you."

"Ross, why didn't you tell me?" she wanted to know.

"Because I was ashamed," he said simply. "Then that night when I told you the truth and it seemed that it didn't matter to you, I began to hope."

"If I'd only known," she said.

"The last few months have been pure hell," Ross admitted. "Loving you, and needing more than anything in the world to tell you so. But I promised you, Dub, that I'd leave her alone and I was honor bound to keep that promise."

"Dang it! I done told you I didn't hold you to a half-baked promise you made years ago," Dub said, flustered.

"I know. After that I had to come up with a whole new slew of reasons why I couldn't love Glory. But what it all boiled down to was a conflict between my shame and my pride. I couldn't figure out how love could fit in that equation.

"After I fired Harvey, I knew I had to leave Oklahoma. So I cashed in my CDs and had the money transferred to my checking account. That's where the money came from."

"I never believed you were involved in Flyer's theft, Ross," Glory said vehemently.

"It doesn't matter now," he said.

She looked up at him, filled with all the love her heart would hold. "No, it doesn't. I'm glad you came home, Ross."

Dub cleared his throat noisily, as if to remind them they still had company. "Well," he said with his typical bluster, "I sure am glad that's settled. You two near about gave me an ulcer worrying about how this thing was going to come out. It was a sight worse'n one of Mama's soap operas."

"Oh, Daddy." Glory hugged her father. "You don't have to worry about us anymore."

"Good. Now we can talk business." Dub pulled out of Glory's embrace and faced Ross. "I meant what I said about selling my interests in Phoenix Farm. Mama and me have had our eye on a little place on Lake Texoma for quite a while now. It'll be a lot easier to leave here if I know it's in good hands."

Dub smiled conspiratorily. "After what you just said, I reckon I might be able to interest my future son-in-law in a little bidness deal. Am I right?"

"Right as rain." Ross's grin was so wide, it made his face hurt. But that kind of hurt felt good. He could have it all now. The kingdom and the princess would be his at last.

"We can firm things up and talk over the figures later, but for right now, a handshake's all I need." Dub extended his hand and Ross gripped it firmly.

Dissatisfied, Dub pulled Ross to him and pounded him on the back. Tears filled his eyes when he said, "Welcome to the family, son."

The two men started talking at once, all about down payments and deferred interest and long-term debts. Finally, having had enough, Glory interrupted them.

"Whoa there, wheeler-dealers," she said with mock testiness. "Just hold on a minute."

Dub and Ross looked at her in surprise. Then they looked at each other and shrugged.

To her father, she said, "A package deal, huh? Is that what this is? The house, the barn, the stock, the daughter? I trust that list is not in descending order of importance?"

Dub looked a little sheepish. "Now, honey—"

"Don't you 'now, honey,' me." She leveled her brown-eyed gaze on Ross. "And as for you, you've neglected one minor detail."

"Which is?"

"I've seen a lot of backslapping, and I've heard a lot of good-ol'-boy negotiations going on. I'm glad you men agree on everything. But I have an interest in this, and what I haven't heard is you asking *me*."

Ross's face reflected his worry. He didn't understand. Hadn't she said she loved him? That nothing else mattered? He felt the dream slipping from his grasp. "But I assumed—"

When Glory realized Ross had misunderstood her, she softened her tone. "Never assume anything with a woman," she said with a seductive smile. "I need a little romance. Vows of undying devotion. I want an official proposal and it better be good."

Ross laughed and Dub ducked out of the conversation, claiming he had to go tell Ruby the good news.

He turned away, leaving them alone to work out the details of the rest of their lives.

Ross and Glory watched the old horseman amble toward the house that they would someday share. The house where they would raise their children. Where they would laugh and cry and grow old together.

Their home. Forever.

Ross pulled Glory into his arms and kissed her with a passion finally freed from all doubts. She felt the heat of his commanding body, the fire of his lips, and her heart raced in anticipation of what the future would bring.

With one finger he tipped her face up to his. "Will you do me the honor of being my wife, Glory Roberts?" he asked in a voice made husky with desire.

"Yes, Ross Forbes. I'll marry you." Glory smiled up at him and saw the promise of endless tomorrows in his eyes.

\* \* \* \* \*

# Diamond Jubilee Collection

## It's our 10th Anniversary... and *you* get a present!

This collection of early Silhouette Romances features novels written by three of your favorite authors:

**ANN MAJOR**—*Wild Lady*
**ANNETTE BROADRICK**—*Circumstantial Evidence*
**DIXIE BROWNING**—*Island on the Hill*

* These Silhouette Romance titles were first published in the early 1980s and have not been available since!

* Beautiful Collector's Edition bound in antique green simulated leather to last a lifetime!

* Embossed in gold on the cover and spine!

---

✂ **PROOF OF PURCHASE**